"You should expect more fr... We should expect more from each other."

"Like what?" A panicked sensation fluttered into her chest.

"I don't know." Only the tick in his cheek suggested this was a more uncomfortable conversation than he was letting on. "But I was serious when I left Toronto, that we need to make a decision."

"You did." She was unable to keep the crack from her voice. "I revealed we were having an affair and you walked away cold turkey." That still hurt. So much. Not a word. *Over.*

He turned another inscrutable expression on her. "Yet here I am, not gone anymore. Am I?"

"Don't." She scowled at her plate. "I don't want to fall into a trap where we're both feeling a sense of loss over Eden's marriage to Remy so we glom on to each other, convincing ourselves there's more between us than there is. I was never going to upend my life for you, Micah. I have plans. And what could you possibly want from me besides sex?"

"I don't know. *You?*" he suggested.

Four Weddings and a Baby

You are cordially invited to...the scandal of the wedding season!

In a shocking turn of events, the marriage of billionaire Hunter Waverly, aka the groom, was halted today when it was revealed he has a secret baby with a local waitress! Their one night clearly wasn't enough...but will this be a real-life Cinderella story?

And the drama doesn't stop there. Our sources say humiliated bride Eden decided to take matters—or should we say, the diamond ring—into her own hands and eloped with best man, Remy Sylvain! Well, those two have always had a special connection since that night in Paris...

Meanwhile, maid of honor Quinn is rumored to have been whisked away by Eden's brother, Micah. And the groom's sister, Vienna? Let's just say, she has the biggest secret of all...

It's never a dull moment at a billion-dollar society wedding!

Don't miss Hunter and Amelia's story in
Cinderella's Secret Baby

Read Remy and Eden's story in
Wedding Night with the Wrong Billionaire

Discover Micah and Quinn's story in
A Convenient Ring to Claim Her

All available now!

And look out for the final installment,
Vienna and Jasper's story

Coming soon!

Dani Collins

A CONVENIENT RING
TO CLAIM HER

Recycling programs
for this product may
not exist in your area.

ISBN-13: 978-1-335-73914-8

A Convenient Ring to Claim Her

Copyright © 2023 by Dani Collins

All rights reserved. No part of this book may be used or reproduced in
any manner whatsoever without written permission except in the case of
brief quotations embodied in critical articles and reviews.

This is a work of fiction. Names, characters, places and incidents
are either the product of the author's imagination or are used fictitiously.
Any resemblance to actual persons, living or dead, businesses,
companies, events or locales is entirely coincidental.

For questions and comments about the quality of this book,
please contact us at CustomerService@Harlequin.com.

Harlequin Enterprises ULC
22 Adelaide St. West, 41st Floor
Toronto, Ontario M5H 4E3, Canada
www.Harlequin.com

Printed in U.S.A.

Canadian **Dani Collins** knew in high school that she wanted to write romance for a living. Twenty-five years later, after marrying her high school sweetheart, having two kids with him, working at several generic office jobs and submitting countless manuscripts, she got The Call. Her first Harlequin novel won the Reviewers' Choice Award for Best First in Series from *RT Book Reviews*. She now works in her own office, writing romance.

Visit the Author Profile page
at Harlequin.com for more titles.

To my husband, Doug, whose shoulder trouble inspired poor Quinn's injury. Thanks for doing such dedicated research for me on this one, darling. I love you.

PROLOGUE

HE WOULD NEVER forgive her for this.

That knowledge stabbed into Quinn Harper's belly like a blade as she announced, "Micah and I have been having an affair. It's been going on for years."

Birdsong ceased and the fragrance of the flowers that surrounded the gazebo turned sour. Quinn was aware of soft gasps of surprise next to her, but all she saw was Micah.

Micah Gould, a man she loved to hate and hated to l—*lust* after. That's definitely all it was, she stressed to herself. She was not a self-destructive person who set herself up for heartbreak. It was lust with a side of long-term friendly acquaintanceship. Best friend's brother with benefits.

Micah didn't move. He had arrived the way he always did, with the energy of a gathering thunderstorm, wearing one of his bespoke suits without a wrinkle or fleck of lint upon it.

He must have traveled with urgency to arrive in

Gibraltar at this moment, but if he was tired or distressed, he didn't show it. He was superhuman that way, always impeccably turned out, clean-shaven and crisp. His short, dark brown hair was only notable because it was thick and absent of a single gray strand. His features were more rugged than handsome and rarely betrayed what he was thinking or feeling.

His expression didn't need to change for Quinn to know he was livid, though. His whole body condensed the way concrete solidified in the unrelenting sun. The way water compressed into a glacier. The way carbon crystalized under pressure to become the hardest substance in the world—a beautiful, icy diamond that could cut through anything.

"Why are you doing this? Now? Like this?" His voice was calm. Too calm. Deadly as a quiet pool that hid riptides and piranhas and bloodthirsty monsters.

"Like this" was in front of his half sister, Eden, who was Quinn's closest friend. And Eden's groom, Remy, Micah's longtime enemy. And Remy's sister, a very innocent Yasmine, still in shock.

The three stood in silence around Quinn, reeling at what she had just revealed.

Quinn was doing this for Micah, not that he knew it. Perhaps he would never fully understand why she was doing this. The layers of secrets were so thick around her, Quinn could hardly breathe beneath their suffocating weight, but deep in the heart of those secrets was a truth so painful, she had to stop Micah from forcing its exposure. He wasn't ready to hear it. It had the potential to destroy him.

If he was forced to realize that Remy's sister—half sister!—was also his own, that he shared a father with Yasmine… If he had to face that devastating reality as Eden married Remy, it might cause Micah to sever the few tenuous threads of family he had, leaving him even more isolated than he made himself.

Someday his father's darkest actions might come to light, but not today. Not when emotions were already fevered and knife-sharp. That ugliness would not besmirch Eden's wedding day. Her *real* wedding day. Quinn refused to let that happen to her very best friend.

Micah looked ready to cause mass destruction if Eden didn't walk away from her elopement with Remy, but the vows had been spoken. If Quinn didn't draw his ire, his feud with Remy would escalate to include Eden and become something that couldn't be repaired.

Quinn calculated all of that in the few seconds following his sudden appearance. She threw herself forward in sacrifice, drawing all the cold loathing Micah aimed at Remy onto herself.

"It was completely consensual," Quinn assured everyone. "I'm not accusing him of anything but appalling double standards. Your sister is allowed to marry whoever she wants." She directed that last statement at Micah. Eden had been pining for Remy for five years. Surely he could see what a lost cause it was to try to stop them?

Micah stared so hard at Quinn, she felt her soul being shredded by the force of it, as though his gaze blasted golf-ball-sized hailstones through her. She had to fight shrinking into herself under that hostile glare.

Then Micah dismissed her in a cold blink that was the cruelest thing he could have ever done to her.

"Are you coming with me or not?" he asked Eden.

"I can't. We're married. I love him."

"He's convinced you of that, has he?" Micah rocked on his heels. His contempt for that particular emotion was thick in his tone. "You can all go to hell, then." He pivoted and walked away.

Quinn watched him retreat, feeling as though her very life force was pulled from her body, trying to stay with him even as he cast her off like a sticky spiderweb that only disgusted him. She swayed where she stood, hollow as an empty shell.

CHAPTER ONE

One week ago, Niagara-on-the-Lake, Canada

SOMEHOW, QUINN WASN'T surprised her maid-of-honor duties included delivering the message that the wedding was off and throwing a change of clothes into a shoulder bag for a fleeing bride. Eden had been very tepid on her groom, stubbornly pursuing marriage for business reasons despite the fact that she was obviously in love with someone else.

When Eden had announced she was marrying Hunter Waverly, Quinn had expressed her concerns, but Eden was her best friend. Ultimately, Quinn supported her. That's what best friends did.

If only Eden had been the one to come to her senses today and cancel of her own accord. No, the wedding march had started when a gray-haired grizzly of a man had charged across the lawn and accused the groom of making a baby with his daughter.

The baby in question had been in the arms of its mother right behind him. That poor woman had been mortified, but the kitten was very much out of the bag. The music was paused, conversations were conducted behind closed doors, and Eden had been thrown over.

Now she was gone.

Conspicuously, she had run away with the best man, Remy Sylvain, which didn't really surprise Quinn, either.

The part where Eden had inadvertently stolen Quinn's car keys was a nuisance, but Quinn wouldn't hold it against her. As rotten days went, Eden was winning first prize. Quinn would accept whatever collateral damage blew onto her.

She peeled off her bridesmaid dress and the shape-wear beneath, then yanked on a drop-waist sundress. She spared a few minutes to wash off her makeup, hating the feel of cover-up more than she disliked her freckles. She liberally applied moisturizer and sunscreen and left her red-gold hair in its updo, but grabbed a hairbrush so she could pull the pins and brush it out in the rideshare car.

As she picked up the notification on her phone that her driver was minutes away, she added an apple to her bag along with a bottle of water and a protein bar. Eden had her own purse and phone, but might want her silk sleep bonnet and that pricy moisturizer she liked so much. Quinn threw those into her bag, drained a warm mimosa, double-checked for her own wallet and phone, then kicked into her sandals.

Outside, the parking lot was busy as a colony of

ants on a barrel of syrup. Between astonished vineyard staff, shocked wedding guests and the sleazy
paparazzi who had trespassed onto the grounds,
word was out that the much-anticipated Bellamy-
Waverly wedding had collapsed. The groom had left
with the mother of his infant daughter. The bride had
fled with the best man—not that that was common
knowledge yet. Quinn was hoping to forestall that
by meeting Eden in Niagara Falls.

"Where are *you* going?" Micah asked behind her
shoulder.

Quinn jolted, not so much startled by his catching
her as reacting the way she always did to Eden's older
half brother. It was an infuriating mixture of joy and
apprehension. A flood of yearning and a reflexive
tension and a need to self-protect. It was sexual desire and abject annoyance because Micah Gould was
too much. Too tall, too confident, too masculine and
too bossy and *so* superior. He was far too capable of
tying her in knots without any effort. The sound of
his *name* tightened her abdomen. His breath on her
neck made her skin feel hot.

She spun around to look at him and that was too
much, too. He had changed from his morning suit.
He had been tagged to stand in as father of the bride,
but now had that European flair that elevated a pair
of raw linen trousers with a short-sleeved camel-col-
ored shirt into something out of an Italian designer's
summer catalog. His shirt was some kind of knit that
hung lovingly off his muscled shoulders. How did he

have the perfect number of fine dark hairs peeking from his unbuttoned collar?

"I'm ready for some peace and quiet," Quinn said. It wasn't untrue. The wedding planner would ensure the guests enjoyed dinner and dancing as scheduled, but Quinn was an introvert at the best of times. "I'll get a room up the road."

"I told you, if you pack her bag—" his voice was silky and lethal as he poked the overstuffed bag hanging off her shoulder "—*I'll* take it to Eden."

"No need. My rideshare is here." She could see a driver craning his neck and waved.

"So you are meeting her."

"Yes. Alone. Not because she was kidnapped—" Micah always assumed the worst where Remy Sylvain was concerned "—but because she doesn't want to deal with you and your elevated testosterone right now."

The car stopped. Quinn leaned down to the open window. "Dave?"

"Niagara Falls?" the driver asked.

"Yes, thanks." She started to open the door, but Micah wrapped his arm around her, pinning her to his side. His size and heat enveloped her as he kept her bent.

She hated how much she loved the feel of his strength as he overpowered her. She could have screamed and elbowed him and made a terrific scene, but he made her weak simply by touching her. She wanted to close her eyes and curl into him and turn her face into his neck. She wanted to kiss his throat and make him groan.

This hold he had on her, both physical and metaphorical, was maddening. It always had been.

"Did you say you're going to Niagara Falls?"

"Yes," the oblivious driver replied. "Are you joining—"

"No. Don't bill her for the trip." Micah dropped a pair of hundred-dollar bills through the window and straightened, pulling her back so the driver could inch his way out of the lot.

"You don't have the right to manhandle me simply because—"

"Are you coming with me?" He released her and walked toward a black BMW.

Quinn knew him too well to stand there and shout at his back. She hurried after him and threw herself into the passenger seat, letting out a huff of annoyance as she buckled.

"He left her at a hotel?" Micah neatly backed out of his spot.

"That's what he said he would do," Quinn said stiffly.

An hour ago, Quinn had realized Eden was no longer at the vineyard. She had called her and Eden had been in Remy's car when she picked up. Quinn and Micah had played tug-of-war over Quinn's phone, Micah performing his overprotective brother act, demanding Remy return Eden to the vineyard. Eden had hung up on them.

A short while ago, Quinn had picked up a text from Eden, telling her she would leave Quinn's keys with the concierge at a five-star hotel in Niagara Falls. Whether Eden was staying there, with or without Remy, was a mystery to be solved when Quinn arrived.

"Why didn't you tell me you were going to meet her?" Micah cut off an SUV and darted onto the main road. He accelerated hard enough she was pressed into her bucket seat.

"Because, in my perfect world, Eden and I will have a good old-fashioned slumber party complete with cheap wine and lots of complaining about men. She just got dumped at the altar, Micah. She doesn't need you showing up to offer I-told-you-sos."

"I won't voice any. I'm the one who gave Sylvain the benefit of the doubt, trusting he wouldn't sabotage his best friend's wedding. I should have insisted Hunter choose a different man to stand up for him."

"As much as I love hearing you admit you're wrong, you're giving yourself too much credit. Hunter has a baby with another woman. I don't see how Remy is at fault for that."

"He wasn't shocked when that woman turned up. He must have had something to do with her crashing the wedding."

"Do you really—" He was so infuriating. "Remy recognized her because he brought Hunter here last summer for a golf weekend. I heard Hunter's sister, Vienna, tell Eden that."

"So Sylvain knew who she was."

"Sure, but are you seriously postulating that Remy arranged this entire thing? That would mean he consulted a psychic last year who predicted that Hunter would meet Eden and decide to propose to her. Then he preemptively took Hunter away weeks prior to that meeting, sabotaged his condoms and somehow forced Hunter to engage in relations with a waitress. You're right. Remy Sylvain *is* an evil genius."

Micah's look swung toward her with the weight of a broad sword.

"*Hunter* is the reason this wedding fell apart," Quinn stated firmly. "Look at the Waverly history. Turning a society wedding into a train wreck is a regular Saturday afternoon for them." Quinn felt a sting of remorse at besmirching Vienna with that brush. She liked her, but it didn't make the statement less true. "Eden doesn't feel it now, but she's *lucky* she's not married to Hunter right now."

"If you didn't like him, you should have told me," Micah said grittily. "Between us, we could have stopped her from taking it this far."

"I am never going to gang up on your sister with you." Eden was the most loyal friend Quinn had ever had. She would never betray her, not even for Micah.

Plus, Eden marrying Hunter would have worked for Quinn in ways that were very selfish and not very honorable, but she kept that to herself.

"Hunter is not a bad person. I think he was going into this marriage in good faith. So was Eden, but she didn't love him." Eden was a romantic and had always wanted to marry for love. "Plus, I don't see the value in marriage. Well, I saw the literal value for her in this one. Obviously." Eden stood to lose her father's chain of stores, Bellamy Home and Garden, if she didn't get an influx of cash, fast.

Quinn hated bringing up marriage and money around Micah, though. She was always conscious of the fact that women threw themselves at him all the time, thinking he was their ticket to both. She'd seen at least two make a play for him at the rehearsal dinner alone.

Whereas she threw herself at him purely for sex and that complicated approximation of affection that he offered when they were between the sheets.

"Given all that Eden was up against, I saw why she thought marrying Hunter made sense. Once she made her decision, I had to support her. That's what friends do. Hunter is clearly a decent man since he put his child first the moment he learned he had one."

"That's where the bar is?" Micah drawled.

"*You* could have bailed her out."

"I *tried*. Our mother refuses to let Eden take my father's money for her father's business. If I could change that, I would. I can't." His hands gripped the wheel so tightly, his knuckles turned white.

He released his frustration by overtaking a couple of cars that were already speeding. The river glittered on one side of them while rows of grapes flashed by on the other.

"Has she been seeing him all this time?" he asked.

"Remy? *No.* When? He was at their engagement party for, like, a minute. He didn't show up at the vineyard until late last night. As far as I know, they've only spoken two or three times since—" She cut herself off, throat always going tight when she thought about that trip five years ago.

"Paris?"

"Yes."

You're a child.

That ancient declaration of his still made her feel so *small.*

"Then why did she leave with him today?"

"I don't know. Eden is my friend, not my preschool daughter. Why do you care who she kisses at a nightclub or catches a lift with?"

"It's not about what Eden does. I'm worried Sylvain is using her to take shots at me. That is what I refuse to tolerate."

Quinn had plenty of experience with people who had ulterior motives. She had learned long ago to spot the opportunists who took in foster children to line their own pockets. Her radar was always alert for shifty eyes and straying hands. She might not have the curviest figure, but from the time her breasts had begun to bud, she'd been subjected to unwanted male attention and the pawing palms that seemed to follow those leering looks.

As naturally suspicious as she was, she had never seen Remy as nefarious. When Eden had met him five years ago, he had casually suggested they join him at a nightclub where he was meeting friends. That was a very normal thing to do.

When they arrived, Remy had tried to include Quinn when he asked Eden to dance, but Quinn had preferred to sulk over Micah dismissing her as a child. Then, after Micah turned up and confronted Remy, nearly coming to blows with him, Remy had kept his distance from Eden for five years. He had seemed prepared to let her marry his best friend even though Quinn had caught him looking at Eden in a way that was both anguished and covetous. Fatalistic and tortured.

It had hurt her to see it and it had mirrored something in Eden's expression when she had told Quinn that, much to her shock, Remy was Hunter's best man.

This was why she never wanted to fall in love! It looked very messy and painful.

But Eden deserved to be loved. She was kind and supportive and had given Quinn so many advantages and experiences she otherwise wouldn't have had. She would do anything for her, even try to get her grumpy brother's buy-in on their forbidden relationship.

"Tell me about this feud of yours with Remy." Quinn began to pick out her hairpins. "His father stole proprietary information from yours and you're still mad about it?"

"No."

"No that's not what happened? Or no, you won't tell me?"

"Both."

Typical. "Fine. Remember this obstructionism of yours the next time you want to know why I always side with Eden." Her friend gave her unconditional love and unvarnished truth. Micah gave her great orgasms and very little of himself.

"I know he's bad news. That's all you need to know."

Because I'm a child?

No matter how much she wanted to sneer that at him, she still cringed when she thought of it.

Still unwinding the twists and braids in her hair, she pretended great interest in the landscape, but she didn't see it. She was thinking about how she had even come to be sitting here, ever grateful for a tiny crumb of contact with this very exasperating man.

Micah loved his kid sister, distance and different fathers notwithstanding. From the time he had reached adulthood and could arrange it, he had brought Eden to visit him in Europe where he spoiled her mercilessly. Eventually, when his work commitments and her desire for shopping and other frivolous pursuits conflicted, he had begun suggesting she invite a friend.

Quinn secretly believed he had been vetting her friendships, culling the ones who hung on to Eden because of her modest celebrity and significant wealth. Bellamy Home and Garden was an iconic

Canadian chain, and one of Eden's grandfathers was a radio personality.

Quinn had met Eden when they were fifteen, both attending a French immersion program in Montreal. Many of the students had booked into it as a chance to get away midsummer. Their parents had sent them for the same reason, but Quinn had been there on a scholarship for the disadvantaged. In the disorder of the registration hall, someone behind Quinn had overheard her being redirected to the desk for "those on financial assistance."

Quinn had earned a pithy look from the student as she turned.

He had given her an up-and-down scan to take in her out of fashion jeans and secondhand top. "They let anyone in, don't they?" he said to the girl next to him. "And *our* parents' taxes pay for it."

"I earned my place on merit," Quinn had shot back in solid French, used to having to stand up for herself. "That's more than you can say, isn't it?"

Eden, standing in the next queue over, had been the only one with enough French to catch the pun. She had burst out laughing.

"*Please* let me be your roommate. I don't want to get stuck with a dud who can't even make me laugh."

Quinn had been pushed around and moved around most of her life. She didn't form solid connections with anyone. She had roomed with Eden and they had some good laughs, but she expected it would be yet another nice but superficial and temporary friendship.

Eden wasn't like that. She checked in and reached out. She stuck.

It had taken years for Quinn to quit being surprised by that and accept that Eden expected them to be friends forever. Thus, she'd hadn't expected Eden's invitation the following summer to come with her to her brother's villa in Greece.

It was such a ridiculous idea, Quinn had immediately dismissed it. The bureaucracy alone was prohibitive. Quinn had still been a ward of the government. Eden was the patient, persistent, anything-is-possible type, though. She had downloaded forms and made calls and somehow all the hoops and barrels were jumped. Quinn had been allowed to go.

Meeting Micah at sixteen, Quinn had been both intimidated and infatuated. He was seven years older and already running a global enterprise that had its footings in robotics engineering. He was rich and handsome and radiated caged energy. His aloof, sarcastic demeanor would have scared the hell out of her if she hadn't seen his indulgent human side with his sister. Eden wasn't afraid to tease him and it made Quinn envious of her confidence in their relationship.

Quinn knew she was on trial as far as he was concerned. She was always on trial in a new house with new people, but she must have passed muster. She'd been invited to ski with them that winter in Saint Moritz. The following summer, Quinn declined Eden's invitation. She had a summer job and was saving for her postsecondary education. Eden visited her for a week in PEI, then took someone else to Micah's London penthouse.

He must not have cared for that friend because he insisted Eden bring Quinn when they met him in Rome the next year, when they graduated from high school. Quinn had only been able to steal ten days, needing to hurry back to the summer job she had lined up, but she dragged Eden through every cathedral and ruin she could find within a few hours' radius before joining Micah in the evenings.

"You genuinely enjoy relics and history, don't you?" Micah said with something like bemusement after she finished an animated description of their day trip to Pompeii.

"I like to learn," she agreed, self-conscious of her enthusiasm. "I find it both frustrating and reassuring that the more things change, the more they stay the same. Two thousand years later, it's still go to work, feed the kids. Visit a brothel." She rolled her eyes.

Micah snorted. "Someone says the world is ending. No one believes him."

"Exactly." When their amused gazes locked, she felt something inside her click.

"You should stay another week." He glanced to Eden, breaking the brief spell. "I'm returning to Vienna, but you could come. There are some excellent museums there."

"You could take us to the opera." Eden smiled slyly.

"I could buy you tickets to the opera," Micah corrected, clearly not a fan. He glanced back at Quinn.

Longing had squeezed her, both for the culture and the time with Eden and the chance to see more of Micah.

"That sounds fun, but I have to get back and start my summer job. They're holding it for me."

"Do you need help paying for school? Let me arrange it," Micah urged. "You're clearly not someone planning to drink her way through freshman year."

"I'm not. You're right." Her chest had filled with the hive of bees that arrived when she was presented with charity. "But no, thanks. I have a scholarship and my dorm fee is included. The summer job is my mad money." If "mad money" included groceries and the cheapest phone plan she could find. "Also, my foster family is being really good to me. They don't have to support me anymore, now that I'm eighteen, but they said I could stay in my room rent-free until I leave in September. I'll go back and help in their garden and with the other kids."

She caught a look that flashed between Eden and Micah, one she feared was pity-related, but Eden said brightly, "Then we'll finally be together for good. We'll tear that campus *up*."

"Oh, yes. I expect our study parties to become legendary," Quinn drawled. "We might live on the edge and put raisins in our cookies."

Quinn had thought she wouldn't see Micah again,

but he always visited Toronto when it was Eden's or their mother's birthday. They had begun including her on those occasions and Micah had personally asked her if she planned to come to Paris with Eden when they finished their first year of university.

"She can run up my credit card all she wants, but I refuse to hold her purse while she sends someone on the hunt for a shorter sleeve. You'll spare me that, I hope?"

"Spare *me*," Eden urged. "He's the worst to shop with. Also, you could finally see the Louvre," she coaxed.

"And the Catacombs?" It was Micah she really wanted to see. Quinn had yet to line up her summer job, but she was too tempted to be sensible. She had agreed to go.

The day they arrived in Paris five years ago, Micah had said to Quinn, "You turned nineteen, too. Put some things on my accounts for yourself."

Quinn had a very complicated relationship with accepting generosity. Coming away with Eden at Micah's expense bothered her, but if she hadn't accepted, Eden would have brought someone else, so Quinn managed to justify it to herself. Buying clothes on Micah's card felt wrong, but Eden would have added outfits for her anyway, so Quinn decided she should at least pick some she liked.

She stuck to simple coordinates that she could wear for school or a job interview, but the quality and tailoring made her feel very grown-up and sophisticated. Secretly, they made her feel as though she belonged in his world.

On their second-to-last night in Paris, Eden took to her room after dinner, fussing over how to do her hair for the nightclub. Quinn had preferred to use the hour to pre-read material for a summer class she was taking online.

She wasn't expecting Micah. He'd told them he had commitments that evening and they'd already eaten dinner alone, but he had suddenly appeared in the lounge where Quinn was curled on the sofa.

"We thought you were out tonight." She tried to pretend her heart hadn't leaped into her throat.

"I thought you two were going out. I'm only here to change into my tux." His attention flickered from her throat to her bare, pedicured toes and back.

Quinn might have made a different clothing choice if she had known he would see her. Her new silk pedal-pushers and striped sleeveless top were smart, but unremarkable. Certainly not sexy, but that glance of his caused a pleasant, squiggling sensation to invade her stomach. Her breath shortened with excitement. Her cheeks stung and she felt both vulnerable and powerful as she held his gaze.

Micah's dark brown eyes were always impossible to read, but she thought she detected heat there. Banked, because he always kept himself behind an invisible wall, but she suspected it would be a conflagration if he ever let it loose.

"Where is Eden?" His voice sounded deeper than usual.

"In her room. Why?" Quinn was riding a wave of sudden confidence in her femininity. "Are you afraid to be alone with me?"

"Of course not. You're a child." His response was whip-fast and stung like the devil.

Considering she had been raised in a series of foster homes without a childhood to speak of, it was a particularly harsh comment. Quinn had been earning money since she was old enough to babysit. Now that she'd turned nineteen, she supported herself, working around her heavy course load so she could eat. She had been adulting as long as she could remember.

His pithy dismissal cut so deep, however, she regressed into a juvenile retort.

"Good thing the *boys* we're meeting at the nightclub are more my age than yours, then." She rose and sent him a look of disinterest as she slipped into her heeled sandals.

"You're *meeting* someone? This morning, you made it sound as though it was a night out." *He* made it sound as though he'd caught her in a lie.

"I didn't say anything." Eden had told him they were going dancing. Quinn hadn't been compelled to fill in any blanks. She felt disloyal at what she had just revealed, but she was also still clapping back at his rebuff.

"Who are you meeting?" he demanded to know.

"No one you'll have to duel at dawn." She deliberately rolled her eyes at him. How did he like being treated like an annoying, interfering adult? "Eden met him at the Louvre the other day. Remy something. He asked us to join him at his friend's club. We meet up with guys at clubs in Toronto all the time." By that she meant virtually never. "I should change. Have a nice evening."

The penetrating way he had stared at her as she walked away had been deeply satisfying. Quinn had flattered herself he was jealous, but that wasn't what it had been at all.

Not. At. All.

"Which hotel?" Micah asked, abruptly slowing for traffic and yanking her mind back to this circus train wreck of a day.

They were entering Niagara Falls, a natural wonder surrounded by high-rise hotels and gaudy tourist traps.

"I don't recall." She pulled out her phone.

"You always recall."

She did have an excellent memory. She also needed to text Eden to warn her Micah was with her. She did that as she told him the name of the hotel.

It was easy to spot, being one of the best situated behemoths with a view of the falls.

Micah pulled into the entrance and handed his keys to the valet, telling him to keep it handy.

"Which room?" he asked Quinn.

"She's not responding." Quinn texted again.

Micah strode to the concierge and asked him to ring Eden Bellamy's room.

A few taps of the keys, then, "I'm sorry, sir. We don't seem to have—"

"Try Remy Sylvain."

"Of course. If you'd like to pick up the extension there…" He pointed at the nearby table.

Micah snatched up the receiver and, when the call was answered, said, "Give me Eden." A pause, then, "Why are you in his room?"

Ugh. What was it about this man and that one?

"He caught me catching the rideshare." Quinn stood close enough to Micah that Eden would hear her through the receiver. "Read your texts."

"You." Micah waved the concierge to approach them. "Tell him to let us up to your room," he told Eden, then handed the phone to the confused young man.

Seconds later, they were striding into an elevator. The young man leaning in to tap his card and push a button.

As the doors closed, Quinn was compelled to ask, "Do you ever stand outside yourself and see what a rampaging grizzly bear you are?"

"This is not a good moment to pick a fight with me, Quinn."

He wanted one, she realized. Maybe a real one.

A grave fear settled over her like a dark shadow. "Micah, please don't be violent."

His cheek ticked. "I won't."

She honestly believed he had not meant to be violent the first time, that night at the club. He hadn't been, but it had been close. He had dragged Remy back from kissing Eden and whirled him around into a confrontation that had descended into shoving.

It was the only time Quinn had ever seen him lose his temper, let alone come close to blows. Thankfully, the bouncers had immobilized both men before anyone was assaulted, but it had still been very unsettling.

The silence in the car on the way back to Micah's home had been deafening.

The elevator doors opened on the top floor. Quinn hurried after him as he strode purposefully down the hall. The room door had been propped open by the inside lock-latch. He shoved in.

Quinn followed and was hit by the same thing that halted Micah.

Nothing.

Eden and Remy had flown the coop. Again.

CHAPTER TWO

MICAH QUICKLY SEARCHED the suite of rooms. It was likely billed as a VIP residence since it was on a top floor and had accoutrements like a bar, a kitchenette and dining area, and a large jet tub placed to allow a view of the falls. He was more interested in the fact that the shower had been used and Eden's wedding gown was abandoned on the chair next to the king-size bed.

The bed appeared unrumpled and he didn't like to spend any time contemplating his sister's sex life, but Remy Sylvain had tried the route of coldly seducing Eden before.

Micah came back to the living room where he took note of the contents of various gift baskets strewn about. The wine in the bucket was open, as was the bottle of scotch on the bar. There was a rack of women's clothing that he assumed had provided whatever Eden was wearing.

He was not a man who gave up, but even as his haze of fury urged him to race back to the lobby to confront them, the thunderous rush filling his ears became deafening.

It was the falls. Quinn had opened the doors to the balcony and stood outside to photograph them with her phone.

It was just like her to make the most of a moment in case she didn't have another opportunity. Over the years, he had learned small quirks like that about her.

Not everything, of course. She was a closed book. Or rather, a set of encyclopedias that appeared unobtrusive at first glance, but brimmed with more knowledge than a single brain ought to be able to contain.

She drove him a little mad for that reason. Most people were obvious in their motives, eager for attention, and were wrong more often than they were right. Quinn was focused, ambitious and understood human nature better than most.

Please don't be violent.

He hadn't planned to be, but that didn't stop a hot brand of shame from settling in the pit of his stomach. Paris had been the closest he'd ever come to behaving like his father. He had actually sought counselling for a time afterward. Eventually, he was reassured that he didn't have the same potential to lash out, but Remy Sylvain still got under his skin in a way no one else did.

Micah knew Quinn thought he was overreacting, but Quinn didn't understand all that Remy had cost him. Maybe Remy felt equally justified in coming after Micah. He, too, had had a taste of Kelvin Gould's temper, but that didn't mean Remy should involve Eden in their conflict. Eden was the most precious person in Micah's life, untouched by the belittling and manipulations that had permeated his own life and that of their mother. He would protect Eden at all costs.

And he had *tried* giving Remy the benefit of the doubt. When he had learned Remy was Hunter's best man, he hadn't interfered, hadn't assumed the worst.

His complacency had come back to bite him, though, hadn't it? Remy kept persuading Eden to go with him.

Why? What did he want with her?

Outside, Quinn lowered her phone to read it. In the car, she'd pulled her hair loose from its complex wedding arrangement. The red-gold strands were frizzing in the humid breeze and the same wind ruffled the hem of her sundress, pressing it to her ass so he could discern the Y shape of her thong.

Be mine, valentine.

A knot of want twisted in his gut, messing with his ability to think.

He tried to tamp it down as she turned and came inside to waggle her phone at him.

"Eden says Remy is taking her to Toronto."

Micah swore tiredly and looked to the door. Did a car chase all the way to Toronto make any sense? No. Not when their mother was still at the vineyard, expecting Micah to drive her home in the morning.

He swore again, hating to lose on any level. This loss was particularly punishing.

"Relax. He's not a serial killer."

"You don't know that," he growled. "Did she leave your keys at least?"

"I put them in my bag."

"Good. Let's go." He moved to the door.

"You go. Eden told me to enjoy the room. I plan to do exactly that." She collected a clean glass from the bar and brought it to the coffee table, where she glugged a healthy pour from the open bottle of rosé.

"Your car is at the vineyard. How will you get back to it?"

"Hitchhike?" She sipped her wine as she moved to flick through the rack of clothing.

"I know you're saying that to wind me up."

"I don't understand why it works."

"Because I *care*, Quinn. You're my sister's best friend."

"Is that what I am?" She pressed the rim of her glass to her mouth, but her lashes lifted to send him a look that kicked him in the chest.

"Did you want to be something more than my sister's best friend?" he challenged.

Her gaze dropped to a blouse. "No."

"No," he repeated. The word tasted sour on his tongue. He wasn't sure why.

They had incredible chemistry in bed, but Quinn had made clear on many occasions that she didn't want anything more from him than sex. Micah was reminded often by his aunt that he should marry and "secure the Gould legacy," but he wasn't ready to tie himself down, either.

He often wondered how he had come to have a secretive sometimes-affair with Quinn at all. Initially, he'd been very suspicious of her.

Eden's wealth and pedigree as a Bellamy, coupled with her soft heart, had made her a target in her teens for users and vapid social climbers. Quinn had been different—a dry-witted orphan with eyes too big for her narrow face. Unlike the squealing girls who wanted to troll beaches for boys, Quinn had persuaded Eden to visit cultural sites and be home on time for dinner.

Cynic that he was, Micah assumed he was being lulled toward a false sense of security. That's why, during their trip to Saint Moritz, when Quinn had behaved very shiftily, passing something to Eden, Micah had presumed it was drugs.

It had turned out to be a feminine necessity. Eden had been mortified.

Why are you embarrassing me?

He had apologized and Quinn had accepted it, but she'd been stoic after that. Micah had told himself he didn't care what she thought of him. Eden was his priority, but the glimpse of hurt and injured pride that Quinn quickly masked had sat on his conscience.

As time wore on, she became the friend Eden most often brought when she visited him—and the one he most preferred. She was pleasant, intelligent and savvy. She was a grounding influence on his sister, not caring for fashion or parties. Quinn was focused on her education, planning a career in social work, but not ruling out politics if that was the best way to make a difference.

Anyone else saying those things would have struck him as idealistic, or too full of themselves. He found himself respecting someone so driven at such an early age, though.

Then, one day, he had walked into his Paris mansion and found a composed young woman whose lithe figure lit such a bonfire of lust in him, he immediately rejected it. She was his sister's friend. A *child*.

She'd been nineteen and mature beyond her years, but still. It hadn't felt right to look at her the way a man looked at a woman.

She had thrown some remark in his face and things had deteriorated further that night, when he accosted Remy. He knew she'd been insulted by his patronizing dismissal of her because she didn't take any of the clothes she had put on his account. She had asked his housekeeper to have them returned instead.

As far as people who held grudges went, Quinn was his equal, which didn't exactly help them get along in the long term.

So leave, he told himself.

She was ignoring him, sipping her wine as she held different items of clothing against her front.

His plethora of responsibilities danced in his periphery, but Eden didn't want his help right now.

She'd run away to prevent him from offering it. His mother wouldn't be missing him. Despite the drama of her daughter's wedding being called off, she was enjoying the chance to catch up with various relatives.

He turned to fix the latch that was propping the door open.

Behind him, he heard Quinn draw a breath as though she was about to say something.

He pressed the door closed and swung the latch into place, then turned to see Quinn rearranging whatever had been in her expression to something more blasé.

"You've decided to enjoy the room, too?" Her tone lilted with amused challenge.

"If you'd rather be alone, say so."

"And deny you the view of Canada's most famous natural wonder? I couldn't."

"I presume you're referring to yourself?" He glanced up from behind the bar where he found a clean glass.

Her cheekbones had gone bright red. Her reddish-blonde brows pulled into a flat line.

"Why do you always assume my compliments are mockery?" he asked with exasperation.

"Because it wasn't a compliment. You were being sarcastic."

And there was the clash. He had thought he was throwing out clever and sincere flattery, but she loved to take everything he said the wrong way.

He poured himself a scotch that he took to the sofa, sitting and propping his feet on the coffee table, far happier to watch her shop than stare at however many liters of water were falling off a cliff.

She continued to glare at him.

"What do you want me to say? That I *don't* find you attractive? I think you'd call that disingenuous."

"I'm pretty sure you find me convenient," she muttered.

Did she really think living with an ocean between them was convenient?

"If you really believe that's all I think of you, then you ought to tell me to take a leap over those falls. You're better than that and we both know it."

She rolled her eyes.

"Oh, am I giving you too much credit? Or is it that I'm *your* convenience?"

"You are many things. Convenient has never been one of them." She gave the clothes a final swish and turned away from the rack in disgust. "You're a distraction."

"*I* am," he scoffed. She filled his head at the most inopportune times. From the moment Eden's wedding had been announced, Micah had been wondering when he would see Quinn. How often. She was his quiet obsession and he would love it to stop.

"If I hadn't been so consumed with getting away from the vineyard without you catching me, I would have remembered to bring my laptop. I could be working right now."

"So I'll take you back to the vineyard and you can work. What are you working on?" he asked with confusion. "Did you get a job?"

"My proposal for my PhD. But I wouldn't get anything done there and you know it." She set aside her half-empty glass and casually stepped over his knee so she straddled his thighs. As she set her knee next to his hip, the hem of her dress rode up, almost exposing her underwear. The cushions sank on either side of him as her weight settled warmly across his legs. "Let's get this over with."

"I don't claim to be a romantic, but even I find that off-putting." It was a lie. His blood was already singing. The fragrance of sunscreen and sunshine and that subtler honey and nutmeg she naturally exuded began to numb his brain. He set aside his glass so his hands could settle on her waist and tug her an inch closer.

"We both know it's going to happen. At least once it's done, we can start behaving like adults again."

He snorted, doubtful, but she was right. This seemed to have become inevitable whenever they crossed paths. Without conscious thought, he was slouching lower and pulling her tighter into his lap. A rough noise rattled in his chest as her heat penetrated his fly and warmed his hardening flesh.

The way her ice-blue eyes melted and her golden lashes drooped was deeply satisfying. He watched her catch her bottom lip, all shiny and pink. He *needed* to suck it.

"Do I need a condom?" He had one. Three, actually. He had anticipated he would be alone with her at some point and had wanted to be prepared.

"I haven't been with anyone else since last time."

"Me, either." He refused to contemplate what it meant that they seemed to say that every time. "C'mere." His voice was a rumble he barely recognized.

Her hands moved from his shoulders to his neck and she slanted her head as she pressed her mouth to his, their connection as effortless as always.

The taste and feel of him swept through Quinn's senses. Much as she'd tried to resist, contact with him had become so intensely necessary for her, it was painful. Why was he the only man to make her feel this way? Sometimes she feared that she had imprinted on him for life. His hands were the only ones she would ever let touch her. His lips the only ones she wanted against her own.

Granted, they were very clever hands and lips. He knew exactly how to pet her, using the right amount of pressure and lazy, precise urgency as he slid his touch down to her buttocks, seeming to savor the feel of her while infusing her with deep pleasure. She was kissing him, but he was the one who made it so compelling. His tongue brushed hers, inviting her to deepen their connection. She did and moaned as she sank into the sheer luxury of being with him like this.

Sometimes she thought a kiss would be enough. That she just needed a taste of him, but it was never enough. Even on a humid day like today, she couldn't get close enough. Couldn't be held hard enough. She wanted to be absorbed through his skin so she was inside him forever.

It was a neediness that brought a sting to her eyes, one that should have had her pushing away from him so she wouldn't succumb to it, but she sank into sensuality and the sense of belonging—not to him, but *with* him. It was only lust, she reminded herself, but there was no place for blunt reality right now. Not when she could wallow in the hungry pull of his lips and the wiry thickness of his hair between her fingers and the thick ridge of his erection right where she wanted to feel it.

Well, almost where she wanted it.

Cool air swept up her back as he gathered the skirt of her dress, sweeping it up her torso. She lifted her arms and he didn't stop until the soft cotton was floating toward the floor. His arms stayed up and he leaned forward. She raked at his shirt, dragging it up and off, throwing it after her dress.

She removed her bra herself while he slouched back and worked on his belt buckle. His thighs pressed hers apart another inch as he opened his fly. He shoved his hand into his boxer briefs, pushing his clothing out of the way to fully free himself.

Oh, she adored the way he was built. Every single bit of him from the whorl at the crown of his head to the soles of his feet. It was pure animalistic instinct to want the most powerful male in the pack, the one with lean muscles that radiated strength and endurance. She let her greedy hands take in all the skin he had exposed—his thick shoulders and meaty pecs, his flexing biceps and his washboard abs. His hot, ever-so-hard erection that pulsed in her grip as she squeezed him and made him groan.

She had an urge to slip to the floor and take him in her mouth, but he swept the backs of two fingers beneath the string of her thong. His knuckle petted and caressed down her center, grazing the sweetest spot, making her breath catch.

A satisfied growl left him. He was watching her through slitted eyes as he did it again, this time with more purpose.

She bit her lip, squeezing him while holding very still for his deliberate touch. When he pulled away, she gave a sob of loss, but he casually snapped the thong and dragged it free, tossing it away before he cupped her mound with his wide palm.

Her body instinctually rocked against his hand, seeking the delicious waves of pleasure and heat he incited. She dipped her head to kiss him again and for long minutes they caressed each other, both of them doing the delicate, knowing things that made it good for the other. She swept her thumb across his weeping tip. He slid a finger deep inside her and his free hand cupped her breast, teasing her nipple until she was quivering in acute arousal.

"You're almost there, aren't you? Take me inside you," he commanded in a voice that was raspy and filled with carnal hunger. "I want to feel it when you shatter."

She wanted to feel him inside her when she shattered. With a small, helpless noise, she shifted higher on her knees and guided him. As the wide dome of his crown pressed at her entrance, he curled his arm around her back and angled his head, capturing her nipple in the hot cavern of his mouth, trapping her high on her knees.

She was so close! He held her there, pulled taut between two points of need, between the draw of his mouth on her nipple and the thickness her yearning flesh craved. She curled her fists into his hair, each breath a ragged flame. Every pulsebeat was a throb of unanswered need.

"Micah!" She dragged his head up and he let her weight press down. His hard flesh slid effortlessly into her, filling her with intense satisfaction as the pressure of his pubic bone took her over the edge.

She threw back her head and rolled her hips, instantly subsumed in orgasm, reveling in the shivering contractions and the way his hands kept her deep in his lap.

As the sharpest waves began to subside, she brought her head up and saw his nostrils were flared, his teeth bared in his effort to hold back his own climax. His fingers dug into her hips and his eyes were glazed with heat.

"See? A natural wonder." He gathered her up and flipped her onto her back on the cushions, the weight of his pelvis settling against hers in a way that brought all her nerve endings back to life. "Now, let me see that again from this angle."

CHAPTER THREE

MICAH HADN'T SLEPT LONG, ten or fifteen minutes tops, but it had been deep and solid. He was naked on the sofa, unsurprised to find himself alone. Quinn always seemed to slip away before they had to look each other in the eye.

The door to the balcony was still open. Mist had condensed on his skin, leaving him damp and chilled. It was a little too depressing for his otherwise physical contentment, but he was too lazy to move.

Quinn was right. He was thinking like an adult again, wondering why the hell he kept doing this with her. It definitely wasn't a convenient affair. They lived on opposite sides of the Atlantic, crossing paths only a few times a year.

Nevertheless, it had become their habit to tear each other's clothes off, then act as if it hadn't happened. That was more her choice than his. He wasn't embarrassed by their affair, but he agreed that Eden would make more of it than it was.

It had started two years ago, when Eden had

finished her business degree. Quinn's major was feminism and gender studies, a topic she was very passionate about—thus her insistence on independence and agency and his extensive education in respecting her choices.

Not that he minded. Much as his inner Neanderthal wanted to say, *Woman. My bed. Stay there*, he couldn't help appreciating how confident and self-sufficient she was.

That's why he'd insisted on including her when he invited Eden to his Greek villa. Quinn had put herself through school and graduated with honors. That deserved recognition.

Things had been unsettled between all of them after Paris, though. Micah had acknowledged and apologized for his poor behavior with Remy before they left, but Quinn hadn't come with Eden the next time she visited. She had been busy with an accelerated track at school, but Micah had still taken it personally.

Perhaps he should have told them that he had sought counseling after acting so irrationally in Paris, but his sessions had been deeply private, forcing him to dredge through some painful memories in his childhood. Today had tested the equilibrium he'd gained since then. He was still angry at Remy for absconding with Eden, but he accepted that she was a willing participant in her abduction. Surely that proved him fully evolved, he thought dourly.

Either way, he had blamed himself when Quinn

initially hesitated at coming to Greece. It turned out she was prepping for her master's degree. Eden had persuaded her to take a week away and Micah had hoped they would get back to the relaxed dynamic where Eden teased him into lightening up and her chatter with her friend made his home less tomblike.

It wasn't like it had been, though. His sister had been an adult moving into a position of responsibility at her father's corporation. She'd been somber, beginning to feel the weight of it.

As for Quinn…

He blew out a constrained breath. Quinn had not been a child, either. She had had at least one boyfriend by then, or so he'd heard through Eden. The earnest biologist had had a manageable amount of debt and a passion for conservation, according to the dossier Micah had commissioned on him.

Much like the handful of men Eden had dated, Micah had shamelessly checked up on him. He didn't think the man was good enough for her, but without any serious red flags, he had had to let her find that out for herself.

Quinn must have come to that realization, because she had broken up with him by the time she touched down in Greece.

Micah had recently ended an affair himself and, given their respective singlehood, Eden had gotten the idea they should become a couple.

"Quinn would make the best sister-in-law you

could give me." She had played it off as teasing, but Micah knew that, deep down, she really wanted it.

Quinn knew it, too, and addressed it head-on when they had a moment alone a few days later.

"Where's Eden?" he had asked when he found her reading on the terrace.

"Salon. Getting her vacation braids." She set down her book, expression serious. "Can I speak to you about something?"

"Problem?" He settled across from her, trying not to notice the way her freckles went down past the scooped neckline of her top where it exposed her upper chest, or the way her legs uncurled as she brought her feet to the paving stones, toes painted neon pink.

"I would do almost anything for Eden, you know that, but I won't marry you," she had announced. "It's not personal. I doubt I'll ever marry anyone."

Micah was used to women presuming they had a shot with him, so he couldn't resist drawling, "You could wait until you're asked."

"That's why I find it so objectionable." Her mouth stretched into a humorless smile. "Why must a woman wait until she's asked? It's a patriarchal institution that only benefits men."

God, he enjoyed when she got all superior and pushed back on him like this. She was the tennis adversary who forced him to work for every point.

"You're making a vast overgeneralization." He deliberately dug into a contrary position. "I'm filthy rich. A woman would gain a very comfortable life, marrying me."

"Doing what?" Her tone was scathing. "My independence is priceless. Can your wealth and wedding band give me that? On the contrary, I bet you'd insist on a prenuptial agreement that would actually constrain your wife even if she left you. Don't pretend that marrying you would gain a woman anything when it starts out with concessions."

"A prenup is a sound precaution. That's a fact. Many would argue it's a chance for both parties to protect themselves."

"It's a contract. Don't call it marriage if it's a business deal. I am happy to consider a business partnership where I'll be treated as an equal, but I won't give up my freedom so I can fulfil an outdated domestic role that immediately gives you the advantage simply because I'm the woman and you're the man."

"Really, Ms. Gender Studies? People aren't locked into such rigid roles anymore. What about same-sex marriage?"

"What about it? Even when there are two husbands, it's still the norm for one partner to become a caregiver while the other is the breadwinner. Marriage promotes inequality. Therefore, no thank you."

"You really believe that? You don't see it as two people bringing a broad array of resources to bear, providing their offspring the best chance at thriving?"

"If you think marriage is the only way babies are made, I have a picture book you'll find very enlightening. Look, if you want to get married and have children, go right ahead. I'm only saying I don't plan to do either."

"You don't want children?" That did surprise him.

"*Want* is the wrong word. I don't intend to *make* children. There are plenty in existence who need a parent. I'll choose fostering or adoption when I'm ready."

Ah. "Sometimes I wonder how someone so analytical and, dare I say, cynical, could be such good friends with a romantic like my sister. Then you say something like that."

"Call me a bleeding heart. I dare you." She narrowed her eyes.

"A soft heart," he amended. "Behind the thick wall of thorns."

"It's a thick wall of cast iron, Sir Kettle."

He snorted. This was also why she was friends with his sister. Even when she voiced strong opinions, she never took herself too seriously.

He enjoyed her company. He always had. In that moment, he couldn't help admiring her as an introspective, self-possessed adult who knew exactly what she wanted out of life.

For just a moment, he let himself wonder if her passion and playfulness extended to the bedroom. How would it feel to be the recipient of her intensity if it turned sensual? Hellishly good, he would bet.

When his gaze climbed from the open button at her throat, her blue eyes were waiting for him. The sexual awareness he had ignored since Paris was suddenly a glowing fire between them, impossible to hide or smother.

Her short lashes flared wide, then fluttered in the briefest moment of disconcertment. Just as quickly, she made up her mind and lifted her chin. One ribbon of red-gold hair sat against her freckled cheek. Her eyes were flickering between the hot center of a flame and the inviting hue of a tropical sea.

"Would you like to have sex?"

For a frozen second, he wondered if she was reading his thoughts.

His scrambled brain tried to find a reason why she was off-limits, but they were consenting adults with an empty house.

Nevertheless, he was compelled to clarify, "Are we still debating the pros and cons of marriage?"

"Are you still expecting me to wait until I'm asked?" Her tone was lightly mocking, but he noted the tension across her shoulders.

This had taken some courage on her part, given the fact that he had rebuffed her the last time she'd acknowledged the attraction between them.

He did not have the strength to do it again.

"You really want to have sex?" His voice had descended to the bottom of his chest. "Why?"

"I believe they're called orgasms," she said with a bland smile.

"I would have thought an independent spirit such as yourself wouldn't need a man for that."

"Too right." She rose. Her mouth was a tight line of indignation. "I'll see what I can manage on my own."

He was on his feet before he knew it, catching at her to draw her back in front of him. He hadn't expected the simple act of setting his hands on her to send hunger sweeping through him, numbing his brain to rational thought.

There was a flash of vulnerability behind her startled gaze, then her hands alighted on his chest like nervous, light-as-air hummingbirds.

"What about Eden?" he managed to ask.

"She won't be back for at least an hour."

Not long enough. That was his basest thought, but, "I mean she'll think—"

Quinn was already shaking her head. "I don't want to give her any wild ideas. This is only for today. We'll keep it between us."

That caused a small schism in his head, but he let it go because if he only had today, only a single hour, he wouldn't waste it talking. He suddenly had a lot of fantasies to explore.

He might have replayed every one of them while he lay here coated in mist off the falls, but an abrupt silence yanked him back to the hotel room.

The sound of running water hadn't all come from outside. Some had been flowing from a tap into a tub and now it had shut off.

Quinn was still here.

Being human was so wonderfully annoying.

There were the decadent man-made pleasures like a deep tub of warm water, the luxury of a tall building overlooking a stunning view, and the cool tang of wine on her lips. Then there was the animalistic fascination that slithered through her when Micah appeared, naked and heavy-lidded, the latent smugness around his mouth reminding her that this languorous bliss in her veins was all thanks to him.

Quinn always felt very raw and defenseless after sex. Anytime she interacted with him, really, but especially after he dismantled her with her own needs and desires.

"Do the jets not work?" His hand went to the dial on the wall.

"I was trying not to wake you."

He twisted the knob and the jets rumbled to life. He entered the tub without invitation, but it was built for two, vaguely heart-shaped so his elbow brushed hers as they settled in their seats facing the view of the falls.

"You're always careful to give me my beauty sleep. Why is that?"

Why did she run away before he opened his eyes? So she could put herself back together before she had to face him again. Today, that would have entailed getting dressed and hiring a car. This tub had been too inviting to resist so here she was, trying to pull her defenses in place while naked next to him.

It wasn't working.

"You always fall asleep. What am I supposed to do? Lie there like a good girl, waiting for you to wake up and notice me again?"

"I notice you," he chided. "Always."

He was doing it now. She felt his gaze on the side of her face like winter sunshine, but only sipped her wine, refusing to look at him.

"Why does it bother you that I said that?"

"It doesn't."

He sighed to the ceiling and splayed his arms across the rim as he sank an inch lower in the water, fingertips close enough to her shoulder to make her skin tingle.

She knew that sigh, though. He thought she was being stroppy and she was.

"Being noticed isn't good," she blurted. "It means you're different. When you're singled out, you're vulnerable. It makes you the prey for hyenas that run you down and rip you apart."

She felt his surprise and the uncomfortable heat of his full attention again.

"Do you genuinely feel threatened when I say you look nice?"

"Do you realize you're looking at me like I'm some kind of weirdo for feeling that way? I wasn't a pretty kid. I was gangly and wore glasses and my clothes never fit. I was called 'matchstick' because of my hair and 'bucky' because of my overbite. Yes. I feel threatened when you comment on my appearance. I'd rather you didn't."

"I didn't know that." He didn't say anything else while, outside, thirty-one hundred tons of water pooled above the falls before plummeting into the mist.

Just as she started to think, *Oh, God, I never should have told him what a freak I am*, he spoke again.

"I don't ever want to make you feel threatened, Quinn." His voice was low, but she didn't think that disturbing rumble in his tone was from the jets rolling against his back. "I can't help being suspicious of Remy, but I won't resort to violence. Not toward him and never, ever toward you."

It was something she had already believed in her heart, but hearing it aloud brought emotive tears to her eyes. She wasn't sure why. Maybe because any promises he made her wouldn't be put to the test of time. They didn't have a future, not really. Not beyond a few more trysts like this one, and those would only come about if she was lucky.

She didn't tell him what she suspected, though— that Eden wasn't simply catching a lift with Remy. Quinn had a hunch Eden would be drawn further into Remy's life and would pull away from both of them. The sliver of space and time that Eden created, the one that allowed Quinn and Micah's worlds to overlap, would disappear. There had been something inevitable between Eden and Remy the first time they had laid eyes on each other. Quinn had sensed it and felt threatened by it. That's how she knew it was real.

"Will you help me understand why you hate him so much? Or at least explain why your mom won't let you help Eden?" This day of upheaval and disaster wouldn't have happened if Eden hadn't been so convinced that Hunter was her only means of saving her father's company.

Micah's expression twisted with distaste. He stole her wine and took a healthy gulp, keeping her glass.

"My father's family—*my* family—" his lip curled again "—were very hostile to my mother when she married him. I can't blame her for resenting them. My grandparents are gone, but I remember them as cold and disapproving. My aunt is very entrenched in the highest social circles and made it very difficult for my mother to make any connections. My father knew how to be charming when he wanted something, but he was a bully."

"Toward your mother?" Quinn asked, thinking of something Eden had told her earlier today. Eden didn't know whether Micah's father had been abusive, but she suspected he had been.

Micah held the glass near his mouth, profile hardening. "My mother has never said outright that he physically hurt her, but he certainly wasn't a kind man, especially after she left him."

It hurt to think of Lucille being treated so badly. Quinn had great fondness for her. As for Micah…

Her heart felt as though it were peeled raw as she asked, "Did he hurt you?"

"I caught a backhand now and again, but he didn't beat me, if that's what you're asking." His gaze went into the glass that he held tilted toward his tense mouth. "I mostly lived with my grandparents when I wasn't at boarding school so I honestly didn't see him that much. I only ever saw him resort to real violence once. Against Remy Sylvain and his father."

"What?" She sat up and twisted to face him. "When?"

Micah swallowed a gulp of wine. "I was twelve. I had finally talked my father into letting me live in Canada with my mother, or so I thought. I started school and joined the basketball team, since that's what all the cool kids did. Remy and I were on opposing teams in a tournament. We had an altercation, as boys do. My father attacked him in retaliation. His father waded in to stop it. They bloodied each other's lips and were kicked out. My father took me directly back to Europe. I resented the hell out of the Sylvains for causing me to be sent back to exile."

"That wasn't Remy's fault. It sounds as though it was your father's."

"Agreed. But why the hell would Remy target my

sister if he wasn't still holding a grudge, years later?" He swung a piercing look at her.

"Because he's attracted to her! I know she's your sister, but she's very appealing, Micah. Men hit on her all the time. They always have."

He only drained the glass and set it aside. "You asked why my mother won't let me underwrite Bellamy Home and Garden. It's because of that. In a thousand ways, my father hurt her beyond her capacity to forgive. He married her when she became pregnant with me, but his parents thought she had done it intentionally to trap him. Their cruelty drove her back to Canada. He refused to grant her custody and gave her minimal access. When she finally had me in her house, he took me away again. She happily cooks for me and occasionally allows me to buy her dinner, but she absolutely will not allow me to pollute the life she made with Eden and Oscar with my father's money."

"That's hard," Quinn murmured. "You should tell Eden. She thinks your mother is being proud, but I get it. Lucille wants to keep ownership of the life she's built. If she lets you step in, it becomes someone else's accomplishment. His."

"BH&G is not hers, though. It's Eden's now. If she makes the decision to accept my help, that will be her own good sense that bails out the company. At least, that's what I've been trying to convince her to see."

Quinn's phone pinged on the shelf where she'd

left it. She picked it up and read the text Eden had just sent.

"Don't shoot the messenger, but Eden isn't going to Toronto. They're in Remy's helicopter, on their way to Montreal." They were heading to Martinique from there, but she didn't get a chance to say so.

"They're *flying*? Damn him!" The water sloshed as Micah stood. Water sluiced off his powerful, naked form and splashed across the tiles as he left the tub.

As much as Quinn would have loved to pretend she was an A-list celebrity on vacation, she was practical enough—and tight-fisted enough—to dry off and go back to the vineyard with Micah.

She didn't linger, though. She packed the rest of Eden's things along with her own and drove to Eden's apartment in Toronto. Eden had offered it to Quinn for the next two weeks, since her plan had been to go on honeymoon with Hunter, then sell this apartment and move into a house with him.

Eden would need it for herself now, Quinn imagined, but at least she had a roof over her head while she searched for a place of her own. Until the semester ended, she'd been living on campus as a dorm adviser, which discounted her rent, making it possible to live on her anemic salary as a teaching assistant while she completed her master's. Most summers she went back to PEI to work and save up for the next year since housing was usually cheaper there, but with Eden's wedding taking up her focus, she had yet to make any decisions about where she would live or work.

To her surprise, Micah turned up the next morning, after dropping Lucille at her home in the suburbs. "Eden told our mother she's taking 'me' time in the Caribbean."

"She texted me the same. I asked if she wanted company," Quinn joked, but Micah was back to oozing resentment.

"I'm sure she has company. Sylvain has homes in both Haiti and Martinique."

"What are you going to do, Raging Bull? Charge down there and tell two consenting adults they're not allowed to have sex?"

"Are they having sex?"

"I don't know! It's none of my business and it's not yours, either."

"Why can't you see my side of it?" he demanded.

"You are knee-deep in hypocrisy, Micah. Would you stop having sex with me if Eden told you to?"

His expression darkened with what she interpreted as dismay. Her heart lurched.

"I'm not going to tell her. Don't worry." She put up a halting palm. "All I'm saying is that sex happens and it's *just* sex. Let it happen so she can move on." She really ought to learn to take her own advice.

"Fine, but if she contacts you, I want to hear about it." He started toward the door.

"What, no goodbye kiss?" she asked facetiously.

He spun around and strode back toward her with such purpose, she stumbled backward and came up against the kitchen island.

Then she was inside the eye of the hurricane. His strong arms surrounded her, dragging her into the storm. His mouth devoured hers, wiping her thoughts clean as he laid claim to her entire being. To her body, with his firm hands running over her, thorough and hungry as he mapped each subtle dip and curve. To her soul, pulling it from her body so she felt empty when he abruptly ended the kiss and stared deeply into her eyes. Into her heart.

"One of these days, we need to make a decision."

He walked out while she stood there, dazed, fingertips pressed to her sizzling lips.

CHAPTER FOUR

Five weeks later

HE *REALLY* WASN'T going to forgive her.

Quinn had expected their affair would be over after her announcement in Gibraltar a month ago. She had expected a cold shoulder from him in future. If she was lucky, he might offer a few heated words the next time Eden had a birthday or some other event they might both attend.

She had not expected him to deliberately undermine her ability to pursue her doctorate. Not when he had always been so supportive of her education. Not when he had sent her an anthology of feminist writings from the seventeenth century when she had been finishing up her master's degree.

But there it was in her email.

Herr Gould has declined to vouch for you. I'm afraid we can't share the letters with you at this time.

"I didn't *ask* him to vouch for me!" she cried, causing one of the other hostel guests to glance at her.

Quinn shook her head to indicate she was fine and scowled again at her laptop, wondering how Micah had gotten involved at all. Yes, she had mentioned him when she was chatting up the volunteer on the help desk, saying Micah had once recommended she visit this particular museum in Vienna. But *she* was the one who had learned they had a collection of letters from the wife of a chancellor to her husband, imploring him to improve the conditions for women and their children in the 1800s. All she had asked was whether she could obtain scans of the originals. Her German was rudimentary and they were apparently written in a Bavarian dialect, but the chance to study a primary source was too exciting to overlook.

The volunteer had said, "Let me check with the curator and get back to you. We've done it before for academics. Your credentials are excellent so I don't anticipate a problem."

Her credentials *were* excellent. Since she hadn't yet found a place to live in Canada, and Eden had flown her to Gibraltar for her wedding, Quinn had decided to seize the opportunity to expand her dissertation research. She dented her modest savings with the cost of a train pass and was buffering the cost of her room and board with whatever field picking or serving shifts she could pick up here and there.

She was really excited about the broader view her

research would allow on her topic and, so far, all the historians in Spain and France had offered her an open-armed welcome.

This museum curator had felt compelled to check with Micah, though. And Micah had put her on some sort of blacklist. What a jerk.

Quinn checked the time, then impulsively placed a call to Lucille. She could have tried Eden, but had a feeling Micah was still ignoring her calls, too.

"Quinn!" Lucille's warm greeting made her smile—and breathe a small sigh of relief. Apparently, no one had told Lucille about Quinn's bombshell revelation in Gibraltar.

"Hi, Lucille. Have I caught you at a bad time?"

"Not at all. I was taking a break from my garden until it's in the shade again. Where are you?"

"Vienna. That's why I'm calling, actually. I wondered if you knew where Micah is right now? I'd love to catch him in person if I can."

"Oh, I can never keep track of where that man will be next," Lucille said. "He's usually on his yacht for the summer, but he mentioned something about his aunt planning a dinner. She'll host that at her villa on Lake Como so if I had to guess, I would imagine he's heading to his villa in Bellagio if he isn't already there. Let me give you his assistant's number. He'll put you in Micah's calendar so you're sure to see him."

Not if he sees me first.

Quinn patiently pretended she needed the contact

details Lucille gave her even as she checked the train schedule to Italy.

"Quinn?" Lucille's shift to something more tentative made Quinn's stomach curdle. Maybe she did know about her affair with Micah. Maybe she disapproved.

"Yes?" She tightened her hand on her phone.

"Will you *please* ask him to call Eden? She's upset that he's still refusing her calls."

"Is he?" At least he wasn't actively sabotaging his sister's future. "I'll bring it up, yes. How are you doing with Eden's surprise marriage to Remy?"

"Still shocked, obviously. It all happened very fast. I already miss having her close by, but I've been to Montreal to see them. They're settling in and seem deeply in love."

"They do, don't they?" Quinn said wistfully. She was tremendously happy for her friend, but felt bereft at how quickly Eden had thrown herself into her new life. This painfully familiar sense of abandonment was another reason Quinn was burying herself in research. She didn't *want* to go back to Canada where her best friend would have so many other priorities ahead of her.

"It was good for the business, too. Remy has been very generous in helping her there," Lucille continued. Her relief that her husband's company was secure again rang strong in her voice. "Eden has her hands full, obviously, bringing things back on course, otherwise I'm sure she'd be on a plane to see Micah herself. He can be so stubborn sometimes."

"Only sometimes?" Quinn asked sweetly.

"You do know him well, don't you?" Lucille chortled.

A sharper twist of yearning went through her. Quinn knew Micah the way she knew most people—by observation. She often wished she knew his deeper thoughts and feelings, but that's not who they were.

"Oh, here comes my neighbor looking for the Bundt pan I offered her. I'll have to go."

"That's fine. Thanks again." Quinn signed off, then pondered her line of attack.

When a knock at the door to his private lounge sounded, Micah muted the headlines he was watching and called, "Come."

"Sorry to disturb you, signore." His housekeeper slipped in and mostly closed the door, then lowered her voice as she continued in Italian. "There's a young woman in the foyer. She claims to be a friend of your sister. She said you might remember her. Quinn Harper? She asks if you have five minutes."

You might remember her. He gritted his teeth at how easily she got a dig in without even being in the room. She had to know it, too.

After the call he'd taken yesterday, Micah had half expected she would make an effort to get in touch. He hadn't anticipated she would show up at his lakeside villa in Bellagio, or that knowing she was in his home would cause his hackles to rise while pouring hot anticipation into his groin.

He did have five minutes, but they'd been ear-marked for exactly what he was doing, nursing a shot of scotch while he caught up on current events before he changed and attended a dinner for which he had no appetite.

Send her away. That's what he should have said. He was coldly furious at the way she'd treated him in Gibraltar. It still didn't make sense to him, but he would be damned if he would beg her to tell him why she had revealed their relationship with such blithe indifference. She always took Eden's side against him, he was used to that, but that's not what she had been doing. She had been defending Remy. Micah couldn't stomach that level of turncoat betrayal, he really couldn't.

The whole episode was so infuriating, he could hardly bear to think of it so he really ought to *send her away.*

"Have her wait in the study." He shot back his drink, savoring the harsh burn down his throat before he took his time rising, then showering and shaving. He dressed in his dinner suit, leaving his white jacket off, too hot under the collar to wear it. He blamed the July heat, even though his stone villa was com-fortably cool.

When he strolled into his study, Quinn replaced a book on the shelf.

She squared herself to face him, brushing whatever dust was on her fingertips against her crinkled blue skirt. Her sleeveless cotton top was ribbed so it hugged her subtle curves. Her sandals were practical walking shoes. A straw bag sat on the floor near the sofa.

She looked the way she always looked to him—like a ballerina poised to flit and twirl and race off stage left. Her hair was rolled into a knot on the top of her head; her aloof expression was clean of makeup. She always seemed very cool and disinterested, but he knew how sensuous she was and that always heated his gut. The way her lips betrayed her mood, pursed now in preparation for making some sharp remark, fascinated him no end.

Her direct blue gaze landed like a punch in the chest.

"Yes?" he prompted when she didn't speak. He steeled himself against whatever apology she might try to make.

"Why did you tell the museum in Vienna to withhold those letters from me?"

He snorted. So no apology, then.

"An acquaintance called to say you were using my name to gain access to their archives. I said you were overstepping our relationship and that I couldn't vouch for your character."

"Really." The tendons in her neck flexed. "You said those words with a straight face?"

"How are you keeping a straight face now?" he

shot back. "After all your lectures on personal choice and agency, you failed to ask my permission before you publicly shared something that you and I agreed we would keep between us. I can't vouch for your character when you no longer have my trust or respect."

She flinched as if he'd slapped her.

He had come out swinging, determined to strike back for the sting of exposure she'd caused him, but he hadn't expected she would go white like that, and grasp at the edge of the bookshelf as though she needed the support.

Alarmed, he took a step forward, but she recovered just as quickly.

Her hand dropped to her side and closed into a fist. She firmed her footing as though bracing for a physical fight. Her mouth became a flat line and her glare, sharp as a laser, sliced him into fillets.

"You're right. I did that. I knew you would hate me for it, but I did it to protect your sister. It's clear you have never really trusted me or you would have known that. So fine. Make my life harder. I don't care what you think of me."

"Obviously," he couldn't resist pointing out, but his conscience twisted. He did know she would do anything for Eden. Quinn was Eden's best friend in the most literal sense.

She might have flinched again, but she had moved to snatch up her straw bag so he missed seeing her expression. She looped the long handles over her shoulder as she straightened.

"I have never tried to trade on my relationship with you. You know that," she said with dignity. "It wasn't even a relationship and this is why. I knew it would end and I knew that when it did, you would be ruthless about severing all ties. I don't care how you treat me. Do you understand that? *I don't care.*"

"Have you ever heard the expression about the lady protesting too much?" He had wanted to hurt her and he had. He could hear it in the strain of her voice and saw it in the brightness of her eyes, but there was absolutely no satisfaction in it. He felt sick with himself.

"Okay, you're right about that, too. Does that feel good?" Her cheeks wore bright spots of red. Her mouth quivered, but her chin was up, her shoulders squared for conflict. "I wanted to believe we could remain friendly once our affair ended. It galls me to hear I've lost your trust and respect, but guess what? *You've lost mine.*"

He snapped his head back, shocked to discover what a heart-punch that was. He was deeply insulted by her icy declaration. "Because I told the truth to a museum curator?"

"Because you throw people away. Go ahead and toss me." She touched her breastbone. "I get that. I never meant anything to you in the first place, but Eden is your *sister.* Do you know what I would do to have one of those?"

The break in her voice cracked against his eardrum. She was blinking fast, chest rising and falling as though she had run all the way from Vienna to confront him here.

"I guess you're so rich, you can afford to throw away one and get another when it suits you." The profound contempt in her bitter words left a pall in the back of his throat.

"Don't make this about Eden," he scoffed as she started to turn away. "You betrayed my confidence. Own it."

"You—!" She spun around and pierced holes through him with her icicle gaze. Her whole body was visibly shaking.

For a split second, he had the sense she was going to say something that… Hell, he didn't know what was about to happen, but he was facing a deadly creature right now, the kind that would strike with poisonous venom or charge and run him through.

He held his breath, tense and waiting, but her voice was eerily calm when she spoke.

"You want to make this about us? Fine. I knew you would find it hard to forgive me. It was a test and you *failed*. More than that, the way you're treating Eden tells me I was right to never envision a future with you. If you can cut your own sister out of your life so heartlessly, what chance would I have had? I did us both a favor, Micah. Say 'thank you.'"

A strangled laugh hit his throat even as she flung open the study door and slammed it behind her.

In two steps, he had his hand on the door latch, but he could already hear the front door opening and closing.

He swore and let his hand fall to his side, not bothering to chase her. What was the point? To insist she was wrong? That he hadn't cut Eden out of his life? He hadn't.

But he was being a stubborn ass toward his sister, avoiding her calls.

What was his alternative, though? Let her try to convince him she'd made the right decision in marrying a man he hated? Invite them into his home and start going on family vacations with them?

He wanted to believe he was taking time to cool down, but he wasn't coming around to the idea. On the contrary, he was clinging to his anger, returning again and again to betrayal and blame because it felt familiar if not good.

It was a test and you failed.

Why the hell did Quinn have to be right? God, she infuriated him when she called him out on his own intransigence.

He pinched the bridge of his nose, starting to see the gauntlet he'd thrown down when he had told the curator that he couldn't vouch for her. He had wanted this confrontation, but Quinn had picked up his tin glove and slapped him across the face with it.

If you can cut her out of your life so heartlessly, what chance would I have had?

Did she *want* a chance? If she did, that was news

to him because she'd always been very adamant that she had other places to be that were anywhere except with him.

"Signore?" His housekeeper tentatively tapped on the door, breaking into his brooding. "The chauffeur has pulled the car around. He's ready when you are."

The dinner party. Micah bit back a weary curse. His aunt worked the levers of society with cold-blooded alacrity, always looking after her own interests, but those included ensuring the Gould side of his family thrived, so she was occasionally useful.

Micah had agreed to meet her grandson-in-law, whom she wanted him to hire into an executive position despite the young man still being wet behind the ears. Micah suspected she would thrust a potential wife under his nose again, the niece or daughter of someone whose favor she wanted to curry. There would be the usual shop talk about a property or project she thought he should consider and she would have opinions on Eden's recent marriage, not that he had any desire to hear them.

It would all be addressed in the space of two hours and served up with a pleasing menu and a carefully chosen flight of wines. She was an efficient and attentive hostess, but those were the nicest things he could say about her.

He shrugged on his jacket and walked outside to his car. The late-day sun was sinking, throwing long shadows. The soft breeze carried the sounds and smells of summer—dry grass and motors on the lake and the distant wail of an ambulance siren.

It all vanished as his driver sealed him into the capsule of the car. Moments later, they crept up the lane and joined the traffic jam on the main road.

The congestion was normal at this time of evening. Micah took out his phone, half thinking to call Eden, but he wanted more time and privacy when he did.

He rolled the edge of his phone against his thigh, corner to corner to corner, pondering how they could get past something that might not be unforgivable, but it was incomprehensible. To him, at least.

Damn Quinn for making him feel so guilty about this!

"I think there was an accident, sir," his driver said. "I see the ambulance is there. Shouldn't be long now."

Micah had a flash of premonition, but reflexively dismissed it. He wasn't the type to make up things to worry about or latch onto them when he did. Besides, he would know if something had ever happened to Quinn.

That was a ridiculous thought. He wasn't psychic and was highly skeptical of anyone who claimed to be.

But his gut was filling with cement. He hadn't heard a car when Quinn left. She must have been on foot or catching a rideshare at the top of the drive? Maybe a bus. He'd never noticed where the closest bus stop was to his home. He had no way of knowing which direction she'd taken as she left, either, but he did know she had been fueled with anger.

Walking fast, she could have reached the intersection up ahead and *why the hell* was he putting himself through this ridiculous exercise?

She was fine. Quinn was always fine. She said so anytime he asked.

"There goes the ambulance. We'll start moving now." His driver crawled forward.

Micah's heart began to crash in his chest for absolutely no logical reason at all.

As they came toward the corner, a policeman seemed to be taking a statement from a woman. The woman offered the policeman something red and white.

"Stop!" Micah shouted.

He was briefly thrown forward as his driver stood on the brake. Micah leaped from the car before his chauffeur could find a place to pull over.

"Let me see that," Micah barked as he charged up to the cop and the woman.

"Signore!" The policeman tensed as though confronting a madman while the woman fearfully offered the phone.

It was exactly what Micah had feared. The screen was smashed to a broken web. The back of the case wore tire tracks across the *I Heart PEI* lettering.

Micah wanted to throw up. His vision tunneled and he thought his knees might unhinge.

"Do you know who it belongs to, signore?" the policeman asked from a thousand miles away.

"I do."

CHAPTER FIVE

QUINN WAS WAITING for the painkiller to kick in, aware that even when it did, it wouldn't fully relieve her agony because not all of it was physical. None of it was particularly new, either, which made it extra excruciating.

Her shoulder was dislocated again. The misalignment in her joint hurt so much she could hardly breathe, but at least she was no longer jostling through the narrow streets of Bellagio in the back of an ambulance. She was in a hospital bed in the emergency room, trying to comprehend the Italian spoken beyond the curtain...*benefici medici* must be something to do with her medical benefits.

She'd given a young woman her wallet. They must have found the card, but it was a low-premium travel plan for students. She doubted it offered much coverage.

The headache of dealing with bureaucracy was already upon her, coupling up with the sting of a shallow pocketbook that had dogged her all her life.

Atop that was the depression of having lost Eden, the one person she might have called in a case like this, but now didn't feel right. Plus, even though she'd thrown a metric ton of superiority at Micah because he wasn't speaking to his sister, Quinn had been dodging meaningful conversations with Eden herself, pretending she was hideously busy so Eden wouldn't guess she was steeped in possessiveness and loss simply because Eden was in love and married and living her best life.

Then there was Micah.

She might have thrown her arm over her eyes in chagrin, but the second she so much as thought about it, a knifing sensation cut across her chest. Hot tears pressed behind her eyes and her throat closed over a cry of pain.

Damn him for cutting her loose the minute she had acknowledged they were together. Damn him, damn him, damn him.

"Signorina Harper?" The curtain around her fluttered. The nurse gave her a compassionate smile. "You have a visitor."

Ugh. His blinding good looks seared into the backs of her eyeballs. He'd put on a white jacket so he was even more crisp and formal and secret-agent sexy than ever.

She closed her eyes against him, the only defense she had right now. *No.* Just *no.*

"You were hit by a *bicycle*?" His tone of outrage was thick with blame, as if she was at fault.

"Apparently, I really am skinny as a lamppost. He didn't see me until I stepped out from behind it."

"And stepped in front of him. Why would you do that?"

"I didn't do it on purpose! I had the signal to walk. The cars were stopped. I thought it was fine." The cyclist had been riding into the sun. He hadn't slowed, believing he could make the turn ahead of the oncoming cars.

He'd been very apologetic when he had stood over her, blood pouring from his chin and knee. He was probably in an adjacent bed, getting bandages hastily slapped over his scrapes, same as they'd given her.

"You're conscious, at least." Micah sounded...

Oh, she didn't want to imagine he sounded relieved or worried or as though he cared one wit.

You no longer have my trust or respect.

Funny how learning she didn't even have that had made her realize she had always yearned for even more.

"Do you have any sense of the severity of your injuries? The nurse said your shoulder appears to be dislocated. Did you hit your head? Anything broken?"

"No. Just my shoulder." And, "appear"? She'd felt it dislocate as the two-hundred-pound man had slammed into her. The impact had knocked her off her feet and the screaming pain had kept her from softening her tumble across the pavement. That had added various scrapes that the nurse had already sprayed with antiseptic and covered. By tomorrow, she would have more bruises than freckles, but she hadn't hit her head or fractured anything that she knew of, so that was something.

"I don't suppose you've called Eden." He set her shattered phone on the table beside her, then took his own phone from his pristine jacket.

"Don't," she said flatly. "I'll call her later."

He scowled. "She'll want to know you're in hospital, Quinn."

"She'll think she has to drop everything and come, but she's busy trying to put her company back on the rails while starting her marriage in a new city. There's nothing she can do anyway. They'll take an X-ray, treat me like a heretic at an Inquisition while they put it back, then wrap it and tell me to be more careful next time."

"This has happened before?" His restless gaze flickered from her cheekbone to the ice pack on the front of her shoulder, down to her limp hand resting on the blanket across her stomach, and ended at the tent of her feet.

"Why are you here?" she asked with annoyance that was a mask for the pain of knowing he hated her.

"To see how badly you're hurt. Obviously."

"I'll live. You can go."

His gaze clashed into hers with the force of a full-on electric storm, making her breath hitch, but the nurse came back with a rake of the curtain.

"I'll take you for your X-ray now." She set a wheelchair by the bed and lowered the rail.

This was going to be a nightmare, one she would rather Micah didn't witness, but she didn't have the breath to say so. With the nurse's help, Quinn very gingerly sat up, blinking as the pain intensified.

Micah stepped forward, reaching out, but she warned him with one raised finger not to touch her. Her eyes were watering and her whole body was shaking by the time she eased herself into the wheelchair.

"I'll wait here," he said grimly as the nurse turned her chair.

"Don't bother." She meant it. She couldn't take him right now, acting like he cared when he didn't. Thank God she had this horrific injury to explain the way her lip was quivering.

By the time she returned to her bed, the drugs were doing their job. She was indifferent to the physical agony and emotional angst of existence. She wasn't indifferent to him, though. To her shame, she was relieved he was still here, even though he radiated the energy of a caged tiger.

"You're shaking," he noted as the nurse got her on the bed and under the sheet.

"I'm cold." They'd helped her change into a hospital gown before the X-ray. None of it had been fun.

"It's shock. I'll fetch a warmed blanket," the nurse murmured.

Micah removed his jacket and draped it over her.

Now the smell of his aftershave was filling her nostrils. She closed her eyes against all the memories his scent evoked—like losing her virginity to him.

She pushed at the jacket. "Don't you have to put this on and be somewhere?" She was seconds away from a full breakdown, she really was.

"I told my aunt that something came up. And I texted Eden that you were here and I would keep her updated. I haven't heard back, but when she sees it, she'll want to know how you're doing."

She was terrible, both dreading and urgent for the treatment. She knew the worst of the pain would subside to a dull ache afterward, but the transition would be insufferable.

The nurse came back, thankfully giving her an excuse not to answer. The woman tucked a blanket around Quinn that was so deliciously warm, she could have wept with gratitude and nearly did.

"The doctor will be along shortly. He's reviewing your X-ray now."

Quinn closed her eyes again, concentrating on her breathing and trying to relax muscles that were filled with flight chemicals, wanting to run to somewhere safe, away from this pain.

It felt like a hundred years, probably because she could feel impatience wafting off Micah every time footsteps passed beyond her curtain without coming in.

Finally, the doctor slipped in, apologizing for the delay.

"I've asked our orthopedic surgeon to consult. She should be here any moment." He brought up an X-ray on a monitor that he pulled around so it was in Quinn's line of sight. "There's a lot of damage here, not all of it from today." He pointed at the image. "There's scar tissue here and this tendon has completely torn away. This has happened before?"

Quinn wanted to lie, she really did. Dredging through the past was her absolutely least favorite thing to do, especially with Micah standing there listening.

"Once when I was nine, once when I was fifteen," she admitted. "But I do all my exercises very faithfully. It hasn't given me any trouble until this happened." *Just put it back and let me go home.*

Or rather, back to her hostel. Ugh. It was going to be a long, uncomfortable night and a hellish flight home that would probably cost the earth once she booked it. She already dreaded however many buses and trains and transfers it would take.

"Were those falls? Or sports…?" the doctor prodded with a concerned frown.

Why was he forcing this?

"The first one happened when I didn't hear my foster father tell me it was time to get out of the pool. He caught my arm and pulled me out." She'd been so unprepared, she hadn't braced herself for the yank on her arm.

There was a choked sound off to her right that

Quinn distantly realized was Micah, but she quickly got out the rest.

"The second time was in high school, when my PE teacher didn't believe me when I said I was afraid I would pop my shoulder if I fell during the tumbling she insisted I try." The teacher had given Quinn some potted daffodils the following week, when Quinn had sat on the bench doing her algebra homework with her wrong hand.

The doctor made a noise of dismay as he looked back at the X-ray. "This tendon needs to be reattached or this will continue to happen."

"I'll keep getting hit by bicycles?"

The doctor only blinked at her. She couldn't even get a laugh right now? That put the cherry on her sundae of misery.

"I can't get an operation right now. I have to go back to Canada," Quinn told him.

"How do you plan to do that?" Micah asked tightly.

"I believe it's called an airplane."

"You can't lift your arm, Quinn, let alone luggage. She'll stay with me while she has the surgery and recovers."

"Fun as *that* sounds, no thank you." She looked to the doctor. "Would you *please* put my bone back where it belongs and wrap me up? I promise I'll see my doctor as soon as I get home."

"Ah. Here's Dr. Fabrizio," he said as the curtain hooks rattled.

A petite woman appeared. She had her hair up and diamonds dangling from her ears. She wore a white coat over what looked like an evening gown.

After a brief introduction, she and the emergency physician consulted in Italian for several minutes, pointing and circling things on the image.

Micah listened intently while Quinn was totally lost. She blamed the drugs, but it bothered her that they were all so serious. When Micah asked a question, their answer made him nod grimly. Her anxiety skyrocketed.

"I agree this can't wait." The surgeon finally spoke directly to Quinn in heavily accented English. "This joint needs to be stabilized and you look to have some nerve impingement from one of your previous injuries. Are you numb on the back of your arm?"

"Sometimes," she admitted reluctantly, not revealing that she couldn't put anything heavier than a hat into an overhead bin on an airplane.

"I have a full roster tomorrow so I'll do it tonight." The surgeon nodded at the hovering nurse, who promptly hurried away. "It might take a little time to get you in, but we will."

"Wait. What? Tonight? That can't happen." Genuine panic began to take over Quinn's system. She looked to Micah, desperate for him to step in and save her.

"You need the operation, Quinn," he said, quiet and firm.

"No, I just need to keep it still for a few weeks, then do my exercises. I've done this. I know what to do."

"Dr. Fabrizio treats some of our nation's top athletes," the original doctor assured her. "You won't find better care anywhere."

This was just like all those times when grownups had made decisions for her without listening, only this time the bill would come to her instead of the government.

"I can't pay for this. Have you checked my insurance? They won't cover it."

"I spoke to the admissions desk while you were getting your X-ray." Micah brushed away her argument with a brisk. "It's all taken care of."

Which was probably why the exalted surgeon had rushed from whatever gala she'd been enjoying to attend to Quinn, but the only thing worse than having to pay for emergency surgery in a foreign country was owing the cost of it to Micah Gould.

"We'll realign the socket, then do the surgery arthroscopically. It's low invasion so it won't affect your healing time too much," the surgeon said cheerfully.

"This way you will only have to go through the healing process once," Micah added before she could protest again. "This has to be done, Quinn." He was using his most implacable voice. "Do it now so it's over with."

It was harsh logic, but she saw the sense in it.

Short of refusing treatment out of belligerence, she didn't really have a choice. That made her chin crinkle in helplessness, though. She didn't want surgery!

She fought tears as she gave a mute nod of agreement.

Micah was not squeamish, but standing by while Quinn had her shoulder set was the worst thing he'd ever witnessed. Whether the pain drugs had helped was up for debate. She didn't scream or cry, but the yelp that escaped her at one point would ring in his ears forever.

So would the knowledge that a man had grabbed her in anger when she'd been *nine*, causing her to suffer to this day.

He had imagined nothing could make him feel so helpless as he had on the way here, not knowing the extent of her injuries. *I'll have to tell Eden*, had been his single grim thought, but he hadn't known how he would do it if the news was truly bad. He'd been unable to breathe until he'd seen that Quinn was conscious.

Then he'd had to listen to the doctors point out issues that should have been dealt with properly in the past. The impotency of his rage on that front was something he had to push aside while he took a fraction of her pain in the form of her nails digging into his hand.

When she released him, he snatched up a tissue and mopped her temples. Tears were streaming from the corners of her closed eyes and she was shaking again.

"It's over now," he tried to soothe.

"No, it's not," she croaked, turning her face away from his attempts to dry her eyes.

She was blaming him for insisting she needed the surgery. She didn't want it and who would? The best he could do for her was ensure she was given the highest level of care, so that's what he was doing. It was a helluva lot better than people had done for her in the past. What sort of teacher bullied a girl into reinjuring herself?

"Was he charged?" Micah asked grimly as they were briefly left alone.

"The cyclist?" She frowned through her haze of drugs and pain. "It was an accident."

"The first man who dislocated your shoulder."

"No. That was an accident, too." That had to be sarcasm, but she closed her eyes again, voice drifting with disinterest so it disguised her real thoughts. "I was moved to another home, though."

As if that was any compensation?

The nurse returned with an IV bag and a tray of instruments. "I have to prepare her for surgery and finish her paperwork now."

He nodded, but didn't move. He'd never seen Quinn look so utterly outdone. The fierce light that usually beamed out of her was firmly doused and it made his veins feel full of grit.

"Is there anyone I can call besides Eden?" It was

disgraceful that he didn't know. At the same time, he braced against hearing she'd met someone in recent weeks.

"The youth hostel on Via Patrice," she said with a wince of discomfort. "They were adamant that they kick you out if you tie up a bed and don't use it. Tell them they can put my things in storage. I'll pick it up as soon as I can."

No one else? Her lack of an emergency contact was actually worse than hearing she had a secret lover he didn't know about.

"Signor Gould?" An assistant with a clipboard caught his eye and motioned that he had paperwork of his own to sign.

He stepped away and the curtain was pulled firmly closed behind him.

CHAPTER SIX

HE DIDN'T SEE her again for hours. The nurse told him there was a delay as they assembled the team and prepared the theater, that Quinn was lightly sedated and resting comfortably, but it annoyed him that she was abandoned like luggage in some prep ward where he couldn't be with her.

He made a number of calls and answered a few emails, then he was stuck pacing the private room Quinn had been given.

The suite more closely resembled a five-star hotel than a hospital room. The bed had a wooden head and footboard and was made up with cheerful yellow bedding and a colorful throw. Mahogany panels hid equipment inside the walls while spring-green drapes covered a window that ran the length of the room.

It was dark, so he left them closed.

Along with two armchairs, there were two dining chairs, a small table, and a kitchenette with a kettle, a microwave and a selection of light snacks in the small refrigerator.

No booze, which was a pity, but he made coffee, feeling as though he'd lived a lifetime since Quinn had shown up in his foyer four hours ago. He kept thinking about that moment when he'd almost gone after her, then let her go. If he'd delayed her by seconds, this accident wouldn't have happened.

It was a test and you failed.

Those words were barbed thorns that dug deeper under his skin each time he tried to pick them out. He wanted to reject them. He was no expert on relationships, but he knew they weren't supposed to be like that, where you set someone up and cut them off when they disappointed you. He was trained to hate failure of any kind. To feel it as deep shame. His perfectionist tendencies were the result of drills, not a true compulsion to be flawless.

If she had told him what the test was, he would have passed, damn it.

Maybe.

It wasn't even a relationship and this is why. I knew it would end and I knew that when it did, you would be ruthless about severing all ties.

He had never expected their affair to go on as long as it did. Their first time was supposed to be their only time. It had been her first time ever, which had shocked him when he had realized. He'd been past the point of no return, buried to his root inside her, nearly mindless with carnal need, but it had penetrated that her tension was more than nervous shyness. It was discomfort, despite her enthusiastic encouragement and the powerful orgasm he'd just delivered with his mouth.

"Why me?" He'd been floored. Humbled.

"I trust you'll never hurt me."

"I just did." He'd never been so overcome with tenderness and chagrin.

"Not that bad." She turned her mouth into his neck.

He'd taken such care with her after that, determined to make it good for her. It had been amazing. Giving her orgasms had been a drug he couldn't quit. Their "only today" had turned into three more stolen opportunities before she left.

Maybe there'd been a part of him that had tested *her* after that. She'd claimed it would be a one-off and he had deliberately not reached out afterward, convinced she would text or call first. He was a wanted man—a bachelor with a fortune—but that had never seemed to impress her.

The complete radio silence from her had dented his ego, if he was honest. Then he'd turned up for Eden's birthday and during a lively round of singing over a cake full of candles, Quinn had leaned over to him.

"Do you want me to come to your room later?"

"Yes." He'd spent the rest of that dinner drowning in anticipation.

His mother's birthday had been the next time, then a New Year's Eve party, another birthday—he couldn't remember whose. They'd even hooked up after Eden's father's funeral. That had felt wrong, but also incredibly right. They were getting good at sex by then, stripping without ceremony and testing the load-bearing weight of various pieces of furniture.

Micah had come to Toronto to meet Hunter when Eden was contemplating becoming engaged to him and it had felt strange to have a family dinner without Quinn at the table. She'd been tied up with her thesis, according to Eden.

Quinn had texted him later that night, though.

You up for a nightcap? I need a break from the books.

She'd only been in his hotel room an hour, but what an hour. They'd barely spoken, consuming each other like animals. She'd been gone when he woke, almost leaving him with the sense it had been a particularly vivid wet dream.

He'd missed Eden's engagement party, which had meant he missed an opportunity to see Quinn. He'd felt it, much to his disgruntlement. By the time Eden's wedding had rolled around, he'd been champing at the bit to see Quinn. There'd been too many social demands at the rehearsal dinner to steal away with her and Quinn had been glued to Eden's side all night.

Micah had stood by, watching a couple of groomsmen and even a winery employee take a shot at her. He'd wanted to shove every single one of those men to the floor, but she hadn't given any of them more than a vague moment of her attention.

She had been waiting for him. He didn't know how he'd known that, but he had.

They hadn't found their chance until they were in that hotel room in Niagara Falls. It had been spectacular, as usual, but he'd been distracted by his sister running away with Remy.

The next time he'd seen her, she'd blurted out their affair like it was nothing worth protecting. He'd walked away from it and her. Furious.

Hurt.

"Signore?" The nurse broke into his brooding. "The doctor said to tell you everything went well and she's in recovery. She'll be brought up in an hour or so."

"Grazie." He pulled out his phone and texted yet another update to Eden, noting it was dinner hour, there. It wasn't like her to be out of touch like this. Had she blocked him?

He started to call their mother, but his phone rang with a video call.

Eden.

His first unsettling reaction was a reflexive desire to hit Ignore. He was still unable to wrap his head around how his half sister could have married a Sylvain. How could she believe herself in love with Remy? As far as Micah knew, until Eden's wedding to Hunter fell apart, Eden had only spoken to Remy a handful of times.

The other reason he'd been avoiding Eden, however, was one he hadn't even acknowledged to himself.

Would you stop having sex with me if Eden told you to?

His sister knew that he'd been sleeping with her best friend. He wasn't prepared for her to tell him how to behave toward Quinn—or for any questions on how he'd already behaved toward her.

That's not what this was, though. She was worried about her friend.

He accepted the call.

Eden was in a robe, her hair hidden beneath a towel, her eyes wide with anxious alarm. She sat up against the headboard of an unfamiliar bed.

"We had his and hers massages and, um, a nap. I just woke up and saw all your texts. What *happened*?"

Honeymooners. He tried not to dwell on it.

"Exactly what I said." He'd sent a few updates as things had developed. "They should bring her up soon, but I imagine she'll be asleep."

"Who?" a male voice rumbled off-screen. Remy.

"Quinn was hit by a cyclist."

"Is she all right?"

"Not really. She just came out of surgery," Eden replied.

"I'll make coffee." There was a rustle as Remy rose and left.

"Thank God you're with her and she's not going

through that alone." Eden touched her brow. "Are you two—"

"No."

It wasn't even a relationship and this is why.

"She came to see me here in Italy. We had an argument, she walked out and…" *I should have stopped her.* "I guess she stepped off the sidewalk as the cyclist came up to the intersection. No concussion or broken bones." Thank God. "She's banged up, though." He'd seen the blood on her clothes and that, too, had given him chills at how much worse it could have been. "As soon as I learned she was in hospital, I came to make sure she got the treatment she needs."

"Thank you," Eden said solemnly.

It wasn't for you, he wanted to say. But he also didn't want to say it.

He sipped his coffee, finding it had gone bitter and cold.

"When she wakes up, tell her to call me. I can come if she needs me to, but you could get her to an airport if Remy arranges a flight, couldn't you? She can stay with us while she recovers."

Micah's heart flared with something like possessiveness. Remy already had his sister. He wasn't getting Quinn, too.

"She'll need follow-ups. I'll keep her with me and bring her when I come for Mom's birthday. Did you know Quinn's had her shoulder dislocated twice before?"

She nodded, quiet and grave. "I did. Yes."

For some reason, that made his chest feel scooped out. He knew that the two had their secrets, but he had always thought they were girlish ones. Crushes and padded bras and which pain reliever worked best on menstrual cramps.

It struck him that Eden knew deeply personal and painful things about Quinn that he had never been privy to. He felt cheated. Or rather, he was bothered that Eden knew how bad Quinn's childhood had been, but he was even more perturbed by the fact that it had been bad. That Quinn had never shared that with him, beyond telling him once that she trusted he would never hurt her. Not that she trusted him, but that she had trusted him not to hurt her. Physically, he realized.

It was a test and you failed.

"Today might have brought up some stuff for her. She doesn't like people making decisions for her. How is she doing? Emotionally?" she asked with concern.

She'd been so fragile, he couldn't stand to think of it.

He swore as he recollected, "Do you know what she said?" He threw himself into an armchair, able to see the humor now. "The doctor said she needed the surgery or this would keep happening and she said, 'I'll keep getting hit by bicycles?'"

Eden released a burst of surprised laughter. "That's on-brand, isn't it?"

He shook his head, exasperated all over again, but his heavy veil of concern lifted marginally. There was something heartening in this—sharing his amusement with his sister over Quinn's cheeky remark. How many times over the years had she been the one to repeat some witty crack Quinn had thrown out? He'd always liked those snippets, unconsciously waiting for them when he talked to Eden because they always gave him a kick.

The way you're treating Eden tells me I was right to never envision a future with you. If you can cut your own sister out of your life so heartlessly, what chance would I have had?

He mentally swore at himself that it had come to Quinn being in hospital for him to reach out to Eden. What if he hadn't left the house right after and seen the aftermath of the accident? What if he hadn't known she was here? He would still be giving Eden the silent treatment and Quinn would be wearing a sling in some dumpy hostel, shoulder causing nerve damage while she tried to book a flight home.

"Listen, I know I've been dodging your calls—" He was ready to own up to his intransigence.

"Hmm?" Eden wasn't listening. She was looking off-screen. "Now? Are you sure?"

"Yes." Remy's deep voice was distant enough from the screen it was hard to hear. "I told her the other day that he still wasn't taking your calls. She said to tell him if it would help."

Tell who what?

"And you want me…? No, I think it will be better from me, but okay…um…" Eden gathered herself with a deep breath. Her body shifted as Remy sat next to her on the bed, but he stayed off camera.

Micah instinctively braced himself, already knowing he didn't want to hear whatever she was about to say.

"I know you're still upset with me for getting married without telling you—" Eden began.

"Live your life," he cut in. "Marry who you want. Do what you want with BH&G. I'm here if you need anything. We don't need a postmortem." That's all he'd wanted to say a minute ago. He would always be her brother, no matter what.

"We *do* need a forensic audit," she said pointedly. "Because I hate that you're angry with me for falling in love, but that's not what I need to tell you. Has Quinn said anything about why she revealed your affair that day in Gibraltar?"

"No," he said flatly, and shot the dregs of his coffee. "We don't need a postgame on that, either. It's late here. I want to get some sleep." He looked to the door, hoping an orderly would arrive with Quinn.

"Don't hang up. This is important," Eden insisted.

Micah bit back a sigh. "Look, Quinn said she was protecting you. I believe her. Okay? She knew I was on the verge of saying something unforgivable. It was your wedding day so she put me in check. I'm not thrilled with the choices you've made, but you and I are fine, Eden. We'll work it out over time. It doesn't have to happen right now." With her asshat of a husband listening nearby.

"We absolutely have to circle back to everything that has been going on between you and Quinn, but… She really said she was trying to protect *me*?" She looked to her husband, who remained beside her off-screen. "Or did she say 'your sister'?"

"I honestly can't remember, Eden. Today was the first time we've spoken since Gibraltar. A lot has happened."

"You haven't talked to Quinn at *all* since then? You were having an affair with her for *years*, Micah. In all the time you've known her, have you come to understand her at *all*?"

She makes her own choices, he wanted to say, but his sister's mouth clamped shut with such disapproval he locked his own teeth together.

"What's between Quinn and me is between Quinn and me."

"Go ahead and believe that, but we *will* come back to it," Eden said sternly. "What you need to know right now is that she wasn't protecting *me*, Micah. She was protecting…" She swallowed and glanced at Remy again before her expression became entreating. When she continued, her voice was very gentle. "She was protecting your other sister, Micah."

"I don't have—" Micah cut himself off as the pennies dropped. Hundreds of millions of them. They landed on him with hard, peppering weight until it was the volume of a mountainside avalanche.

* * *

Quinn's shoulder was throbbing, pulling her from slumber. She released a discontented sob of frustration and was yanked fully awake by Micah's rasped voice.

"Pain? I'll get the nurse."

His footsteps walked away while she blinked at the palatial room dimly lit by a single golden lamp and pale dawn light coming through the crack in the drapes.

Damn that man. She couldn't afford this.

She looked down at the sling she wore. It wasn't the simple kind she'd worn in the past, but a number of straps that tied a padded pillow to her hip. Her forearm rested upon it while her upper arm was snug against her rib cage. Wonderful. This was going to make life easy.

A night nurse came in to say, "The anesthetic from the surgery has worn off. I'll adjust the drip with your pain medication."

She checked Quinn's pulse and temperature. Quinn was already arranged in a half-sitting position. She offered her a few sips of water before she helped her use the bathroom.

Micah was still there when she came out. He still wore his suit, minus the tie and jacket. His sleeves were pushed up his arms, but otherwise he was his commanding self.

She quickly averted her gaze, feeling weak and pitiful, shuffling around so shakily.

"What time is it?" Quinn asked as she carefully settled back on the bed.

"Four thirty-seven." The nurse tucked the blankets around her. "You have lots of time to rest before the doctor does her rounds." She nodded at Micah and left.

Micah continued to loom on the other side of the room. It didn't make sense that he was here. It made her want to see significance in it when she already knew there wouldn't be.

"Have you been here the whole time? Oh, God, did I say something stupid when they brought me in here?" She had no recollection of it, but did have a sudden flash of those emotional videos online of people coming out of anesthetic, crying and swearing and saying revealing things.

"You only woke up enough to help shift yourself onto that bed, then went right back to sleep. Eden was disappointed. She was hoping to talk to you."

Eden. That was it. Despite what Quinn had said about how he was treating Eden, he loved his sister and, for her, would stay with her friend, even if he no longer liked said friend.

Quinn didn't want to think about their argument or what she would owe him after this. Sometimes you had to accept help from people who held you in contempt. She had survived it before and would again. She would get through all if this and live to fight another day.

Maybe. Now that she was awake enough to assess

it, she was dangerously close to crying over the mess she'd landed in. She was tired and hurting, broke, and a very long way from home. She didn't have Micah as a lover anymore, or even as a friend. Her education, the one thing she had always told herself no one could take away from her, had been undermined, not just by him, but also by her own clumsiness in not looking properly before she had stepped off the curb. How was she supposed to continue her dissertation now?

She really didn't need him watching her have an emotional breakdown on top of the rest of what he'd witnessed today. She opened her mouth to tell him to go home, but noticed how haggard he looked.

Maybe it was the pale light that made his expression seem so devastated, but his eyes seemed sunken into dark bruises. The lines bracketing his mouth were deeper than she'd ever seen them. Stubble shadowed his jaw and his hair was not the smooth cap he usually wore.

"Have you slept at all?" she asked, flickering a glance at the way he'd angled an armchair to use one of the other chairs as a footstool.

"No."

"Why not?" *Was* he worried about her? Her heart lurched.

"What—" He cut himself off and ran his hand over his face, then gave his hair a disgruntled scrub. "What did she say to you? In Gibraltar. Yasmine," he clarified.

"What?" Quinn's heart lurched again.

His distress wasn't about her, then. It was never about her. She should have realized that.

She ignored the squeeze that compressed her lungs and used the excuse of adjusting the sheet to avoid looking at him.

"I'm not sure what you mean," she prevaricated. Her heart quivered with apprehension.

"Eden told me she's my half sister, Quinn. She said that Yasmine found out the day she joined the three of you in Gibraltar. She said Yasmine was still in shock and went across to your room when Eden and Remy had gone to theirs. She told you everything, yes? That's why you threw our relationship under the bus, to keep me from finding out she was my sister before she was ready for me to hear it. What did you think I was going to do to her? Blame her? *Hurt* her? I'm not like him!" He swore and pushed his finger and thumb into the corners of his eyes, muttering, "I work so damned hard not to be like him."

"Oh, God, Micah," she breathed, instantly aching for him. For Yasmine, too, and for Remy who had carried the secret of his sister's conception for years.

"You weren't in a fit state to hear it," she said gently. "You know you weren't. With Remy right there? You thought he was conning Eden out of her company by marrying her. You weren't ready to learn this entire war started because your father did something heinous to his mother. So yes, I changed the conversation. I admitted you and I had sex. Big deal."

"I'm the only man you've ever had sex with. It is a big deal." He was practically shouting and pointed at the floor.

She rolled her lips inward, surprised he'd put that together and more than a little chagrined that it was true.

"Look. I won't betray Yasmine's confidence, but the things she said were just processing. Everything she had thought she knew about herself took a sharp turn so she had a lot to work through. She was curious about you, though. That's why she talked to me. She wanted my take on what kind of person you were."

"What did you say?" His hands went into the pockets on his trousers. His posture seemed tense.

"Nothing personal. I told her that even though I've known you a long time, I don't know you that well—"

"Really," he scoffed.

"It's true," she insisted even as her throat grew dry. "We don't exactly share secrets."

"You knew this secret about *me* before *I* did." His finger pointed about, assigning blame to invisible people for that. "Why the hell wouldn't you tell me yourself?"

The crack in his voice fractured her heart.

"When?" she asked helplessly. "You weren't in a mood for explosive revelations when you arrived in Gibraltar. I've texted you three times since then, asking if you wanted to talk."

"You almost told me today. Didn't you?" he challenged.

She had. It made her cringe with shame.

"I was tempted, but I was angry. This news isn't a weapon. I know it hurts to hear it, Micah. That's why I took one for the team at Eden's wedding."

"Whose team?" he muttered, and rearranged his features with his hand again, still spitting out curses under his breath. "Remy told Yasmine I wasn't speaking to Eden so she told them to tell me. What am I supposed to do with this information? My father assaulted their mother. No wonder their whole family has been out to get me all these years. What if there are more children out there?" His hands went up as if that had just occurred to him.

"It's a lot," she murmured. "But you can't make sense of it if you're exhausted. You need to sleep."

"I can't." He paced a few steps, scrubbing his hair again. "I'm too keyed up."

"Well, I can't sleep with you hovering like the grim reaper. Go home." She wasn't supposed to sleep flat yet, but she was a side sleeper so lowered the head of the bed a little and shuffled, trying to get her good shoulder under her a little.

Micah came to stand over her, hands on his hips, shoulders sloped with defeat.

"What? You paid for the bed so you want to share it?"

"No. I want you to stay up and fight," he admitted without heat. "I'm still really angry with you for hiding the truth and saying what you did without asking me first. But you need your sleep so yes. If you're sleeping like that, there's room on this side."

"You're unbelievable. You know that?"

"I know what you're like, Quinn. If I go home, I'll come back to an empty room and I won't see you until Eden's baby shower." His voice was gruff, but he was infinitely careful as he dropped his shoes and settled in behind her.

She didn't deny that she would absolutely leave if she could. Or admit that having him behind her like that created a nice, warm brace for her to lie back against. He curled his arm under her pillow and she snuggled deeper into the crevice he created.

She had always wanted to sleep with him, but had invariably claimed she didn't want to get caught in his room. In reality, sleeping together was too intimate. It was the ultimate vulnerability. The ultimate bonding exercise. Lying close with him like this was comforting and made her feel like he would keep her safe forever.

Which was an illusion.

"Why did they let you stay all night here?" she asked truculently.

"Because I told them to."

No doubt.

"Comfortable?" he murmured.

"Mm-hmm." She was fighting inexplicable tears.

Why would he insist on staying with her? Really just to fight? Or softer reasons?

She didn't want to think he felt more than an obligation toward a woman he sometimes slept with, though. She didn't want to imagine and hope and believe in things that would never be true.

"Good night, then," he said.

She closed her eyes and matched her breathing to his, mind soon blanking into sleep.

CHAPTER SEVEN

"Oh!" The nurse's gasp woke Quinn.

Micah, too, judging by the small jolt that went through him and the way his arm twitched, then eased from beneath her pillow.

"How are you feeling?" the nurse asked cheerfully as she yanked open the drapes and allowed light to pour in.

"Like I've been hit by a bicycle, missed two meals, and I'm not allowed to shower."

She'd been feeling really nice all snuggled into Micah, but he was already pulling away, rising and rolling his shoulders.

"Breakfast will be here shortly. Then the doctor will come by to discuss follow-up and when you're likely to be discharged. Let me remove your IV, then I can help you in the bathroom, if you like."

"I can manage. I've done this before." There was still a lot of pain, but it was the pain of fresh stitches and healing. It would kill her to admit it, but she was glad she had the surgery behind her rather than in front of her.

"Your things are here," Micah said in a gravelly morning voice. He set her bag from the hostel on the bed.

"How did you get that?"

"My driver picked it up on his way to fetching my own bag." He collected a small duffel and disappeared down the hall.

At least she had her own toothbrush and would have some of her own clothes to change into when she was discharged. Her laptop was here and everything.

Feeling almost cheerful, she gave her face and teeth a clumsy scrub, then ran a brush through her hair. She would have to buy a couple of hairbands to keep it off her face. That always made her look more like Anne of Green Gables than usual.

She came back into her room with one arm through the robe and discovered Micah had shaved. What a monster. He had a clean shirt and smooth hair and was removing the covers from two plates on the small round dining table.

"That's just mean," she said as she sat down across from him. "I had to brush my teeth with my wrong hand. I couldn't even put my hair up."

"I like it down. Don't bother," he forestalled, holding up a hand as she opened her mouth. "I know you don't exist to please the male gaze. Sue me for thinking your hair is pretty when it catches the sun."

Like now? The sun was streaming through the massive window, warming her through the robe she was half wearing, but he couldn't possibly think she looked like anything but washed-up seaweed in this state.

She kept her gaze on the fresh fruit and muesli, pastries and cheeses that had been revealed. "I have never seen hospital food like this."

"I ordered it last night. My driver brought it up as soon as I texted."

Of course he did.

"I appreciate it. Thank you." She filled her plate with the easiest items to eat one-handed, too hungry to be proud. "And I will pay you back for all of this."

"That's not necessary." He poured two cups of coffee and set one in her reach. "You wouldn't have taken this side trip and wound up injured if I hadn't interfered in your research."

"I made the choice to come here, Micah. This is not on you."

"You were upset when you left yesterday."

"I was upset when I arrived."

"We both know I was a bastard to you. Let me apologize," he insisted. "I did believe you were protecting Eden in Gibraltar when you revealed our affair. I have always appreciated your loyalty to her, but she was with Remy. *With* him. He has always been a sore point for me. When you did that, I felt pushed out. Ganged up on. That's no excuse for my interference between you and the museum, though. That was beneath me."

"I should have taken more care to protect your privacy. You have every right to be angry with me. I won't do anything like it again," she promised with a pang in her throat, keeping her eyes on the strawberry she was stabbing.

In the thick silence, she swore she could hear him wondering exactly what she wouldn't repeat, *The affair? Or the exposure of it?*

"I'll talk to the museum, ensure you have full access going forward," he said.

As an olive branch, it was kind but... "I won't need it. This is going to slow me down so I'll go back to my original proposal for my dissertation and go home." She nodded at her bound shoulder. "It's not as ambitious, but Cs get degrees." She had never been graded less than a B-plus and those were an F as far as she was concerned, but as the song went, she couldn't always get what she wanted.

"You would never be able to live with half-assed effort," he scoffed, giving her a funny feeling in her chest at how well he knew her.

"True, but I can't be a student forever. I thought I could push myself through a few more years of full-time school to get my doctorate, but it wouldn't be the end of the world if I worked for a few years and picked away at the degree. The downside is, I wanted a fighting chance at making policy changes once I got into social work, rather than being one of those people who can see what's wrong, can see how to fix it, but doesn't have the power or credentials to push for change."

"That's your end game? Fix the system?"

"Nuts, right?" She knew how pie-in-the-sky that was. "But what's the alternative? Not even bother to try?"

He studied her the way he did sometimes, like he was seeing her. Seeing *into* her.

She swallowed, remembering that they actually hated each other. She'd forgotten that, briefly, and had talked the way she used to, when he asked about school and her plans for her future. When she felt as though they were equals in some ways. Never in all ways, but intellectually, at least.

"I'm not important so I want to do something important," she said with pithy self-deprecation.

His frown deepened, but thankfully, the surgeon entered, putting an end to his intense scrutiny. Or rather, now it became focused on him listening to the details of her reconstruction, asking pointed questions about her follow-up appointments and the physiotherapy she would need.

"I'll do all that at home," Quinn insisted. "I'm clear to fly, right?"

"I'd prefer to do the follow-up myself," the surgeon said, flickering her thickly lashed brown eyes at Micah.

Quinn bet she would, especially as Quinn's desire to rush back to Canada made it clear she wasn't involved with Micah.

"Where are you going to stay when you get back to Canada?" Micah asked with impatience, as though she was being unreasonable. "With the newlyweds? You can't live alone. Not when you can't cook or even get groceries. You can't work. You might as well stay and continue with your proposal for your dissertation. My place in Vienna is walking distance to the museum."

"I can't type." She could actually, and she could also write decently wrong-handed. She'd had enough practice, but she didn't want to owe him more than she already did.

"Use dictation equipment. I have some if you don't want to buy your own." His frown told her to find an argument with legs. "Let Dr. Fabrizio continue your care. I'll take you home when I fly to see my mother for her birthday. What day would you like to see her again?" he asked the surgeon.

Quinn only went along with the arrangements because it meant she was allowed to put on clothes and leave. Of course, she couldn't carry both her straw day bag and the small backpack she was using for travel. Micah had to carry the bigger bag down to the car for her. He handed it with his own to the driver of a BMW, then helped her into the back seat.

"You can drop me at the youth hostel," she said as Micah came in beside her.

"Give us a minute," he said as the driver started to take his position behind the wheel.

The man murmured something in Italian and closed the door, then moved to stand a short distance away.

"You and I said some cruel things to each other yesterday. Maybe we even thought we meant them. At the time." Micah turned his head and his mahogany eyes held indecipherable swirls and shadows. "But we have a lot of history. I can't cut you out of my life. It simply isn't possible."

The bottom of her stomach wobbled, unsure how to interpret that.

"No matter how big a snit you and I get into, you have my promise that you can always come to me for any reason. Put me in your phone as an emergency contact," he ordered, then seemed to recollect, "The phone I will get you because yours was run over. Call me if you need money. A dry bed. Anything."

She was so moved, she thought her throat would close up completely, so she did what she always did when emotions got too much for her. She cracked a joke.

"What about hiding a body? Because I can't manage a shovel right now and the man who ran me down has really ticked me off."

He stared at her for one, two, three heartbeats. Then the corner of his mouth twitched.

"He's already in the bottom of the lake." He looked forward and knocked on his side window to get his chauffeur's attention. "I missed dinner with my aunt and now I have to reschedule."

Quinn bit her smile as she looked out her own side window.

CHAPTER EIGHT

EDEN TEXTED HIM *AGAIN*, so Micah walked into the lounge where Quinn had sat down to catch her breath when they'd arrived back at his villa.

She might sound chipper, but she was still drugged up and sore all over. In the time it had taken him to explain to his housekeeper that a room should be prepared, Quinn had tucked herself into the corner of a wingback chair and had fallen fast asleep.

He'd thought about carrying her up to a bedroom, but aside from worrying he would put too much pressure on her shoulder, he liked that he was able to walk in here and check that she was breathing and comfortable.

It had been nearly two hours, though. He brushed his knuckle against her soft cheek and watched her eyelids flutter in confusion.

"If you sleep much longer, you won't sleep tonight."

"I beg to differ." She straightened and winced, yawned. Her hair fell in her face and she brushed it away, but it wasn't in a mood to behave. "Those painkillers could drop a bull elephant."

She wore one rolled-back sleeve of his shirt, since it had been the easiest item for her to put on around the contraption she wore. Her bottoms were her own boxer-style pajama shorts in pink and green. She should have looked ridiculous, but he had to tear his eyes off her bare legs and the freckles peeking from the open collar of his shirt.

"Eden is desperate for proof of life." He didn't have Quinn's credentials or he would have set up the new phone that had arrived. He offered his own. Eden's number was at the top of his recent calls so she only had to touch the button to place the call. "I'll let the housekeeper know you're up and need lunch."

"Thanks." She took the phone and it connected as he reached the door.

"Is she— Oh, it's you!"

"It's me," Quinn said sheepishly. "I'm fine. I look like twenty miles of dirt road, but I was only knocked, like, ten feet."

"Don't make jokes. You *scared* me. I'm so glad Micah was there. What if you'd been stuck in a hospital and I didn't even know?"

That question had been repeating in Micah's head all this time, along with a thousand other thoughts and reactions to news about his other sister. He'd been agitated last night after that news. Freshly furious with his father—he'd been angry with that man his whole life—and deeply chagrined at the hostility he'd shown toward Remy. Eden had explained that Remy's family had been worried Micah's father would try to claim Yasmine if he knew about her. They'd hidden the truth of her DNA even from her, but all that meant was that his father had yet again dodged taking responsibility for his actions. It fell to Micah to do it.

And there was Quinn, knowing that intensely private information about him, holding it in and navigating his anger while she protected his sister. He hadn't known how to make sense of that, of the fact that he was grateful she hadn't let him do anything stupid, but also furious that she hadn't told him. Why was she always on someone else's side, never his?

Which was a childish reaction, he knew, but in the fraught midnight hours, he'd wallowed in that sense of betrayal, drawing deeply on the pain of it because in some ways, that was the way he understood close relationships were meant to be—painful. As a child, he had loved his mother and sister, but wasn't allowed to be with them. The family he was allowed to see were critical and cold.

When Quinn had told him to go home, he'd been hurt by it and tempted to go. He'd been exhausted and wanted to lick his wounds, but he simply couldn't leave her there. Couldn't risk coming back to her having disappeared.

There was irony in the fact that Quinn always said they could think better after they'd slept together because he'd woken far more clearheaded once he'd slept with her head numbing his biceps and her ass against his hip for a few hours. They had a lot to talk through, but he had the patience now to take it one thing at a time.

Then she'd started talking about going home and compromising her goals and that had been a hard no for him.

In fact, she was probably conspiring right now with his sister to get on a plane, he realized.

He left his instructions with the housekeeper and arrived outside the lounge in time to hear Quinn saying, "Micah has offered to let me stay at his place in Vienna, but I haven't decided."

Maybe *she* hadn't, but he had.

"Are you two…"

"No." Quinn sighed. "This is why we kept it off your radar. We didn't want you to think this was anything serious. It was just…something that happened sometimes. It never meant anything."

"I know you better than that," Eden admonished. "Listen, if you're letting my brother treat you as if you don't mean anything, then I need to have a talk with him. You should expect more from him."

"He's giving me exactly what I want," Quinn insisted. "I don't want to get married and have babies. That's fine for you," she hurried to say. "But I don't want those obligations and responsibilities. I want an education and a career and sometimes I want to sleep with someone. Micah gives me that without trying to take over my life. Why is that wrong?"

"Because you deserve to be loved, Quinn."

"You love me. Don't you? Or are you mad about—?"

"I'm not mad at you for sleeping with my brother. I'm mad at him for taking advantage of you."

Micah's throat tightened with affront.

"I am not that vulnerable," Quinn grumbled.

"From where I'm sitting, you damned well are," Eden shot back.

Micah saw it now, too. He'd always let himself be blinded by Quinn's confidence and saucy comebacks. She was so ferociously independent he'd been fooled into believing she had her entire life under control.

She had very few resources, though. She had health, which had been compromised with this injury, and her education, which he had also impacted.

"Would you *please* stay out of it?" Quinn pleaded.

"Fine." Eden wouldn't. He could already hear the lecture she was planning on giving him. "But Remy is sending you a voucher that will basically get you on any available flight to Montreal. You can stay with us as long as you need. Or use my place in Toronto. I haven't sold it yet."

"I'll bring her home when I come for Mom's birthday," Micah said, striding into the room.

Quinn's gaze whirled up to his, surprise and self-consciousness in the blue depths.

Yes, he transmitted with his steady stare. *I was listening.*

"Quinn wants to do some research in Vienna," Micah stated. "Don't you?"

Her face twisted with indecision.

"You're not a quitter, Quinn. Finish what you started," he pressed.

Another flash of startlement struck her expression. Something that dipped her chin as she tried to read what he meant by that. He wasn't sure what to make of his double entendre, either.

"We have to say goodbye, Eden," he said. "Lunch is ready on the terrace."

Quinn had stayed with Micah in the past. She knew how he lived, so she shouldn't have been surprised at the fine cuisine that was placed before her: handmade tortellini stuffed with crab coated in a saffron sauce. It was accented with olives, bocconcini balls and roasted cherry tomatoes in three colors. The final touch was a sprig of fragrant basil.

Maybe what surprised her was that it was all easy to eat with one hand. Had that been Micah's instruction? Or was his housekeeper that attentive?

"You're not eating?" she asked.

"I ate earlier." He sipped what looked like a Bloody Mary and sat with his introspective profile aimed at the lake.

She wasn't allowed alcohol while she was on the prescription-strength painkillers, but she sure would love some, especially now when she was so disconcerted. Any other time she had been in one of his homes, she'd been more Eden's guest than his and her friend had provided a buffer between them.

Even when they'd been sneaking around, having sex, Eden had been a convenient excuse to maintain some boundaries.

She reached for her friend again, purely because she didn't know what else to say.

"I'm glad you and Eden are speaking again."

"Me, too." His tone dripped sarcasm, probably because he was still coming to terms with the Yasmine news. He snapped his head around, pinning her with one of his most penetrating stares. "Do you think that's why she married him? Because of—"

"No. Wipe that from your mind. Eden loves Remy." A little schism in her chest felt offset by that fact, but it didn't change the veracity of it. "I know it seems fast and very... Eden. She sees the world through rose-colored glasses, absolutely. But she was eating her heart out for five years after meeting Remy in Paris. It's the same for him."

"That's lust. You and I had that, but we didn't make any hot runs to Gibraltar."

Had.

Quinn subtly breathed past the hard lump that lodged in her throat. She looked at her plate, but her appetite was gone.

"We only wanted to share our bodies, not our lives," she pointed out quietly. "What they have is different. It was love at first sight."

After a pause while he seemed to absorb what she'd said, he dismissed it. "Please don't start sipping whatever it is Eden's drunk on. I expect more from you. You don't believe in love any more than I do."

"I don't believe in marriage," she contradicted. "Love is real."

"How can you not believe in marriage? Marriage is real. Marriage is something Eden is now stuck in. Love is an illusion. It's pheromones. It's something a woman tells herself has happened to her when she finds herself pregnant and is scared out of her wits to tell her parents. I'm talking about my mother," he clarified shortly.

"You don't think your mother loves you?"

"We're not talking about that kind of caring, are we? My mother said she loved me, but I still had to leave with my father, so it's not some all-powerful force. Love is just a word, one that looks pretty on greeting cards. It has about as much substance as a piece of painted cardboard."

"Wow. I knew you were cynical, but okay." At least she knew where she stood—in the opening of an icy, bottomless cavern.

He only sipped his drink.

"Regardless of what you believe about the true nature of their feelings, they're married. You'll have to accept that, same as I have," she said stonily.

His eyes narrowed. "If you believed she was in love with him all that time, why didn't you put a stop to her trying to marry Hunter?"

"First of all, she was pretty adamant about marrying Hunter. And honestly? I didn't see a path for her and Remy. Not given how you felt about him. Plus, I knew if she married Hunter…" She bit her lip, but she wanted it off her conscience. "This doesn't make me look very good," she acknowledged glumly. "I knew if she was married to Hunter, she would still need me. Which I know is selfish," she hurried to add. "But she's kind of all I've got. I'm happy for her, though. I genuinely am."

She chewed on a cheese ball, feeling small as she awaited his judgment of her petty, needy heart.

"I have the same sense that he's trying to take things that are mine," he admitted, lip curled in self-deprecation.

"Hmph." There was no real humor in her snort. "I sometimes think you and I have all the wrong things in common. We're possessive. Pigheaded."

"Broken."

"What?" She took that like a knife to the stomach and sat back to absorb it.

"You said it first," he muttered, working his thumb in the dew on the glass he loosely clutched.

"When?"

"When they brought you back to your room last night."

"You said I didn't say anything stupid!"

"It wasn't stupid. It was correct."

"I'm so embarrassed." She set down her fork and tried to hide behind her one hand.

"I know you were stoned off your face, Quinn. I didn't take it to heart."

"What exactly did I say?"

He sighed. "Nothing incriminating. You were glad that I was still there and wanted to hug me, but you were upset that your arm wouldn't work. You thought it was broken and said, 'Why are we both so broken?' I had just ended my call with Eden and was wondering the same thing."

What she'd said was awful enough, but she made herself ask, "Did I say anything else?"

"Why? What are you afraid you said?"

"Nothing." She picked up her fork and shoved another tortellini in her mouth.

"Eden is right," he muttered, looking out to the water. "You should expect more from me. We should expect more from each other."

"Like what?" A panicked sensation fluttered into her chest.

"I don't know." Only the tic in his cheek suggested this was a more uncomfortable conversation than he was letting on. "But I was serious when I left Toronto, that we need to make a decision."

"You did." She was unable to keep the crack from her voice. "I revealed we were having an affair and you walked away cold turkey." That still hurt. So much. Not a word. *Over.*

He turned another inscrutable expression on her. "Yet here I am, not gone anymore. Am I?"

"Don't." She scowled at her plate. "I don't want to fall into a trap where we're both feeling a sense of loss over Eden's marriage to Remy so we glom onto each other, convincing ourselves there's more between us than there is. I was never going to upend my life for you, Micah. I have plans. And what could you possibly want from me besides sex?"

"I don't know. *You?*" he suggested.

Her heart turned itself upside down and inside out. Did he not realize this wasn't anything anyone had ever wanted? Not really? Look at her.

She swallowed and said sincerely, "What we had was very good, Micah. We made some very nice memories and I'm glad we're ending on good terms. That's all anyone can expect from life, don't you think?"

She made herself look at him, but her eyes were hot, her facial muscles tight beneath the blank expression she was trying to hold.

He was staring at her so hard, she felt it as a laser that penetrated to the pit of her stomach. It made her shift uncomfortably, giving her the most awful feeling that he was disappointed in her.

But didn't that prove her point?

A firm, feminine voice sounded in the house, speaking Italian. The words grew in volume as they approached the open doors to the terrace.

Micah swore under his breath and rose. He took a step toward the doors, but a woman was already striding out and across the stone pavers, designer heels clipping in a way that meant business.

She was a stunning woman of sixty-odd years with coiffed silver-blond hair and a complexion like creamed honey. She wore a pastel green sheath with a matching green blazer trimmed in black.

"Aunt Zara," Micah said, polite, but frosty. "I wasn't expecting you."

Oh, snap. Quinn rose and pushed her company smile onto her face, certain this would be awful, but she wouldn't have missed it for the world. Micah had never, ever let Eden meet any of his Gould relatives. Quinn was highly curious.

"You should have." Zara offered her cheek for the buss of his, then sent a distinctly appalled look at Quinn's taste in fashion. "And you have a house-guest. Micah should have included you in my invitation last night. Zara Von Strauss." She held out her hand in a way that forced Quinn to come to her.

"Quinn Harper." She shook the proffered hand, recognizing this particular air of passive-aggressive superiority. Recognizing that it was a blatant lie that she would invite a penniless orphan dressed like this to sit at her table with her family and friends. "Micah was helping me last night. I was in hospital."

"How kind of him." Her smile was a stretch of painted lips. Nothing more.

"Quinn is a close friend of my sister's," Micah said, sideswiping Quinn's heart with that designation that distanced him from anything more personal between them.

She couldn't really blame him, given all they'd been through lately, but it was hard to keep an un-affected look on her face.

Strangely, Zara seemed to stiffen in an effort to hold her own aloof expression as she turned back to Micah. "Here I thought you were evading your responsibilities to family."

"When have I ever?" Micah asked mildly. "Would you like to sit? I'll order coffee."

"Another time, thank you. I won't interrupt your lunch." Another disparaging look was thrown at Quinn. "But we need to discuss a few things while you're in town."

"I'll be tied up with Quinn, then I'm due in Berlin for the Innovation and Design Awards. I've sent tickets to your grandson. I'll introduce him to our executive team. I'm sure more than one will be eager to coax him into their department."

The boss's grand-nephew? No doubt.

Zara struck Quinn as the type who liked to micromanage, though. She wasn't entirely pleased that Micah was leaving her grandson to sink or swim, but she had to accept Micah's action with a satisfied nod and a cool, "Thank you."

"I've also told my property agent to touch base with yours, to review the assessment of the property you've recommended. You've never steered us wrong. I'm sure things will proceed in due course. Was there anything else?"

This was like a tennis match between greats, the undercurrents thick, statements served and volleyed with powerful returns.

"Someone I wanted you to meet." Aunt Zara was

not cowed by the flash of warning in Micah's gaze. "You'll need an escort for the award ceremony."

"I never have before. Quinn will accompany me if she's up to it."

"Oh? How nice." It was not nice. She was livid at the thought. "I won't take up any more of your time. It was lovely to meet you, Ms. Harper."

"And you, Mrs. Von Strauss," Quinn lied.

"Will you walk me out?"

"Of course," Micah said, ever the gentleman.

"Your sister recently married," Aunt Zara said as they strode through the lounge toward the foyer. "We haven't had a chance to discuss that."

"There's nothing to discuss. As you said, she's married."

Aunt Zara's mouth pinched, but she knew the rules where Eden was concerned. That's why Micah had invoked her outside, to warn her against insulting Quinn to her face or behind her back. He had made clear a long time ago that he would not stand for any criticism of his mother or sister.

It hit him that, at some point, he would have to reveal to Zara and the rest of his father's family that Yasmine existed. They were going to have a collective stroke.

"It's charitable of you to help your sister's friend." She never used Eden's name. "I can't fault your loyalty to family." Her smile was chilly. "But you have responsibilities to *all* your family, Micah. Everything you do affects us. It reflects on us. Kindly remember that."

"How could I forget when you're so diligent about reminding me?"

"A young man may enjoy his amusements. A man your age needs to secure his dynasty," she asserted. "You need an heir, Micah. And a wife who is an asset to the entire family."

Oof. He wanted to take her arm and walk her out to hear what Quinn would say about a woman being an "asset."

"Is she really accompanying you to the award ceremony? Like that? Please let me send my stylist, if so."

"'She' has a name. I'll take care of everything Quinn needs," he assured her stiffly.

"Hmph." She offered her cheek and said her farewell.

He stood there a moment after closing the door, recognizing that he'd always known he would have to marry and produce an heir one day. It had been made clear to him thousands of times, especially in the last few years, but he hadn't seriously contemplated marriage because...

Truthfully? Because he'd been keeping himself available for Quinn. It hadn't been a conscious decision. He simply hadn't been interested in anyone else. Aside from setups like being seated next to someone eligible at his aunt's table, he hadn't even dated.

He couldn't imagine spending his life with one

of those socialites she pushed at him. They were always attractive and well-educated and eager to do "good work" for a charity, but he'd never met any who possessed a spark of real personality. None lit a fire in him the way Quinn did.

He'd never considered Quinn for the role of his wife because she'd always made it clear she wasn't interested in marriage and babies.

What could you want from me besides sex?

That, he realized. Marriage. The babies were negotiable, but in terms of sharing his bed, waking next to her and bickering over breakfast, she was already his preferred partner.

He pondered that as he walked back outside, briefly alarmed that she wasn't at the table, but she'd only wandered to the water's edge where she was crouched, feeling the temperature.

She glanced up when he joined her.

"I wish I could swim, if only to wash my hair."

"I'll wash it." For better or worse, he thought with irony. Was he really going down this road?

"Don't be silly." She tipped slightly, trying to stand.

He caught her good arm and steadied her under her elbow, helping her rise.

"I'm very serious." He was talking about more than a hair wash, but marriage was a conversation that would have to be handled with care. She was in no shape to hear it now, still half-drugged with painkillers.

"What would Aunt Zara say to you playing la-dies' maid?" She widened her eyes in mock scandal.

"Aunt Zara is a snob. She drove my mother away, but she understands now what a mistake it is to at-tack people I care about. If she or any member of my family treats you in a way that is offside, you'll tell me immediately."

Quinn tucked her chin, smirking in a way that suggested he was overreacting, but her expression shifted as she realized he was not joking.

That seemed to disconcert her, being lumped in with "people I care about." She rolled her lips to-gether and looked to the water.

"I feel privileged to have met her."

He choked slightly.

"Not like that." Her grin flashed. "No, I asked Eden once what your relatives were like and she said she'd never met any of them. Now I have."

"It's true. For my mother's sake, I've always kept a firewall around Eden, not letting any of my Gould relatives play their mind games on her. Zara just tried to bait me into criticizing Eden's marriage. She still believes the story that Remy's father stole from mine."

"Oh." Her brow pleated with empathy. "That's going to be complicated, isn't it?"

"Tell me about it," he muttered, realizing he wanted this, too—her immediate comprehension of his problem. He liked that she understood his complex family dynamic without him having to show her all the skeletons and label them.

"I shouldn't have said you were broken." She looped her good arm around his and briefly hugged it. "You're split in half. It's different."

"Torn and frayed." Definitely losing his concentration. He could feel the soft give of her breast against his elbow. Impure thoughts bled through him.

He gave in to temptation and let his arm curve around her lower back, mostly because he'd been moved when she'd been so upset last night, so filled with despair that she couldn't hug him. It was one of the reasons he'd wanted to sleep next to her, so she'd be comforted.

So he would.

His hand thought about wandering down to her ass, but he only aligned her a little closer, very gently, under his arm.

Marriage to her could work. He knew it could. He only had to make her see that.

She looked up at him, wary of this casual affection. Uncertain what it meant.

He wanted to kick himself for ever going along with keeping their affair a secret. For only coming together with her in passion, not basic companionship.

"This is good, you know. This injury of yours." He nodded at her sling.

She choked. "Oh, yeah. That's what I've been thinking this whole time. It's great."

"I mean that it's good we can't fall back on having sex to avoid talking about things that are hard." He closed one eye in a wince. "I heard it as I said it."

She chuckled, but stepped away. She always stepped away.

"Do you *want* sex?" She was looking at the water, not letting him see her eyes as she spoke with breezy but vague interest.

"With you? Always. I would think that was obvious." A waver of uncertainty tipped into his chest. Everything he'd been thinking in the last few minutes slid down into a jumbled pile. Maybe he'd killed whatever she'd felt toward him when he'd quit on her so summarily in Gibraltar. "You?" he asked.

She drew a deep sigh and let it go, like a balloon deflating. "Yes."

"You're so good for my ego," he muttered, but she was very grounding, never letting him take himself too seriously. "What I'm saying is, titillating as the clandestine hookups were, it's good that it's not an option right now. We'll have to use our words."

"Ew. No, thank you." She cast him a grimace.

"Coward."

"It's my deepest, darkest secret. Now you know."

She wasn't a coward. That he knew. But she was afraid. Afraid of being alone, afraid of having no say over herself or her future, afraid of revealing her heart.

Looking at her was like looking at a cracked, distorted reflection of himself.

"Come." He jerked his head. "Let's go wash your

hair. It will be fun. Like a team-building exercise."
Maybe they couldn't make love, but he would still
get to touch her.

"Are you saying hair washing is something you
do with your executives at retreats?"

"Before the pillow fight and s'mores, yes. Let's
go."

It took them longer to figure out the "how" than it
would take to actually wash her hair, but eventually Quinn found herself propped on a padded bench
pushed up against the edge of a claw-foot tub.

Rolled towels softened the curved lip of the cast
iron so she was as comfortable as it was possible to
be with her head hanging back into the tub and a
shirtless Micah leaning over her, hairy chest inches
from her face.

"Is that too hot?" He used the handheld spray
nozzle to wet her hairline.

"It's fine." She closed her eyes, but she could
smell traces of aftershave emanating from his jaw
and discerned the heat of his skin radiating toward
her.

He took his time dampening her hair, picking up
the length and squeezing the water through it before he squirted some lime-and-sea-breeze-scented
shampoo onto his palm.

What on earth was he doing? He smoothed the
shampoo across her wet hair in little dabs, then gently began rubbing it into the tresses before piling it

all together while he slowly worked up a lather. She was never this fussy. Soak, scrub, go. She used whatever was on sale when it was time to buy shampoo, combed it out and let it air-dry.

"Oh," she murmured as he began a swirling massage with his fingertips against her scalp.

"Did that hurt? *Did* you bump your head yesterday?"

"No, it feels really good," she murmured. "How do you know how to do this?"

"It's what they do when I get my hair cut." His thumbs worked against her temples.

"Your barber does this?"

"I've started seeing a woman in Berlin."

She snapped her eyes open.

"She gets in here…" His strong fingers dug into the tension at the base of her skull while she stared at his Adam's apple.

As tension released, she groaned, "Oh my God," and let her eyes flutter closed again.

"You're a train wreck, aren't you?" He tenderly attacked the muscles in the back of her neck, using the soap like oil to lubricate the long strokes of his fingers against the tendons before he edged back toward her scalp and turned her whole body into melted wax.

She wallowed blissfully, finally compelled to tell him, "This is better than sex."

"You're making the same sounds."

"Don't make this weird."

"You started it."

She kept her eyes closed, but smiled. She liked when they were like this, when his hands were on her and their jabs at each other were playful and teasing.

When he began to rinse out the shampoo, he asked quietly, "Will you tell me something?"

She opened her eye, suspicious. "Is this still a pajama party? You're supposed to say 'truth or dare' first."

"I dare you to tell me the truth."

"Cheater. What?"

"How many homes were you in?"

She clamped her eyes closed. "Why do you want to know?"

"I don't know." He began to work a tingling, brightly scented conditioner into her hair. "I've been thinking about how angry I was with Remy. I did blame him when I thought I was finally going to live with my mother and sister only to wind up back at boarding school, but the reality is, I didn't hate boarding school. At least I wasn't living with my father or my grandparents. I was in the same boat as the rest of the boys. They were mostly the same boys, year after year, so I knew what I was going back to. I imagine it's harder to walk into someone's home and be the only new person, to have to figure out what the rules and dynamics are. I've been wondering how many times you were put through that."

"It's not that hard once you're used to it. Use your manners, do your chores, finish your homework. Probably all the same rules you had to abide by." She kept her eyes firmly closed to hide that it had been a hellscape of anxiety, every single time.

"So you don't want to tell me?"

"Eleven." *It's just a number,* she told herself, but it felt very damning, as though it marked her in some way. If someone had truly wanted her, she would have had a home for more than a year and two hundred and fourteen days, which was her record for her longest stay anywhere.

If she could have, she would have sat up, but she was stuck in this position, tied by his hands buried in her hair, unable to get away from his tender touch or relentless curiosity.

"From the time you were how old?"

"Four."

His fingers stopped, then restarted.

"At least my mother lived with me until I was six. I still saw her a couple of times a year and talked to her often. What happened to your parents?"

"Boating accident. My grandmother was babysitting me when it happened." She rushed through the details. "She couldn't raise me. She was really old. I saw her sometimes, at first. Then she died."

"There was no other family?"

"None that wanted me."

He swore under his breath. "I'm sorry, Quinn. That's really rough."

"It is what it is." She had had to accept that. "Sometimes my birthday wish was to stay in the house I was in, sometimes it was to leave. Eventually, I realized it didn't matter what I wanted. Things happened the way they happened regardless."

That's why she was so obsessed with having her own say over her life. That's why she wanted to fix systems that continued to push children around like objects rather than people.

Micah didn't say anything as he rinsed her hair squeaky-clean. He dabbed the droplets of water from her cheeks and forehead, then wrapped her hair in a towel before he helped her sit up.

"Stay there," he said when she started to stand. "I'll comb it out."

"You don't have to." She was feeling very weak and shaky despite only lying there, passive.

"I want to."

She would struggle to do it herself, but she was feeling very exposed. No one had ever wanted her. That was her real, deep dark painful secret.

She made a joke to deflect from how raw she was. "You really do have fantasies about being at a girls' pajama party, don't you?"

"Every heterosexual male does, I assure you," he drawled, settling behind her on the bench, splayed knees bracketing her hips.

As he set the comb against her hairline, she said, "Pro tip, start at the bottom. Otherwise, I'll have a rat's nest here." She chopped into the back of her neck.

He did and she watched him in the mirror. His expression was intent as he carefully picked the tangles from the tails of her hair.

"Do you know what I keep thinking about?" he asked as the comb climbed higher.

"I think we've established it's pajama parties."

"Besides that." His expression was very solemn. "I keep thinking about when you said yesterday that I was so rich I could afford to throw away one sister and get another." His gaze crashed into hers in their reflection. "How much do you hate me for having two when you don't have any?"

"I don't." She dropped her lashes, throat cinching tight. "I'm just jealous."

"Don't be." He squeezed her good shoulder and set his forehead against the back of her damp hair, as though hiding from his own reflection. From his conscience. "I still don't know what to think of it. Her. I think about you, wishing you had even one sister, and I know I should welcome this news, but I'm deeply ambivalent. And embarrassed that I feel this way."

"Oh, Micah." She cupped his jaw, urging him to lift his face as she turned her head to look at him over her shoulder. "You're allowed to have feelings. And they don't all have to be neatly organized and pretty."

His mouth twisted. "Are you sure? I thought it was our thing that we didn't allow those messy, unpleasant things."

"It's *my* thing to refuse to do that. You can."

"Mmm." His mouth pulled to one side in dark

humor. It was such a nice mouth. Vaguely wicked in the way the corners were so sharp while his bottom lip was full and carnal.

She licked her own lips, inviting...

"We're not supposed to do that, either," he chided softly.

His attention was on her mouth, though, she saw when she glanced into his black-coffee irises.

"It's just a kiss." She twisted a little more.

He met her halfway.

And yes, this was what they did so they didn't have to suffer the agony of existence, but the agony was always right here, buzzing in her lips, filling her with yearning. It was in the groan that rumbled deep in his chest as he slanted his head and captured her lips more fully.

It was in her shoulder, when she instinctually started to twist and reach for him. Lightning shot through her left side. She jolted and sat straight, breath zinging in her lungs.

"Okay?" His hand splayed on her waist, ready to catch her if she tipped.

"No more spin the bottle," she said in a strained voice. "I think it's time for popcorn and a movie."

A pause of surprise, then, "What do you want to watch?"

"Something where teenagers beat the system by dancing."

"I'll assume that's a dare," he drawled. "I'll go along because I'm a good sport. Also, you're due for another painkiller so I assume you'll fall asleep ten minutes in."

It was twenty, but he watched to the end because she was leaned against him and he didn't want to wake her.

CHAPTER NINE

THE NEXT FEW days passed in a blur, probably because Quinn napped more often than a newborn.

When she wasn't sleeping, she was arguing with Micah—and losing.

"Set up this phone for yourself," Micah said, handing her the latest model, still in its box. She'd started shopping for a refurbished one, but he said, "You and Eden text too much for me to be the middleman."

Her mistake was in acquiescing to that, not wanting to be a nuisance. He seemed to take that as a green light because more goods quickly arrived.

"Your laptop is too old for the latest dictation software," he said when a young man turned up with a new one and wanted to configure it for her. There was also a headset and an adorable little dictation recorder that Quinn secretly fell in love with, especially after the tech showed her how easy it was to speak her notes into it, then set it to auto-type into a document while she walked away.

She would have stopped there, but Micah ordered clothes.

"You need things that are easy to manage," he said, as if she was the unreasonable one when he had hired a stylist who brought a selection of original pieces from *Milan*. "You're in no shape to sift through boutiques, trying things on. When you're feeling better you can buy your own things. Let Antoinette outfit you for now."

Quinn did tire very quickly, and her best clothes had been donated to the hospital incinerator. Aside from pajamas, she had a pair of holey jeans that she couldn't fasten and a T-shirt that claimed feminism was her second favorite F-word. The new clothes *were* easy and comfortable, so she gave in.

Then the private nurse arrived.

"Are you kidding me? I don't need a private nurse," she marched into his den to inform him, leaving the middle-aged woman blinking in confusion behind her. "Sorry," she added over her shoulder. The woman seemed perfectly nice and must think Quinn was extremely ungrateful. "He didn't tell me he had hired you," she explained, then turned back to Micah. "*Why* did you ask her to come?"

"You said you were tired of the sponge baths. I would be happy to help you bathe, if that's what you prefer." His steady look promised to soap all nooks and crannies very thoroughly.

She didn't bother calling his bluff because she knew it wasn't one. Instead, she blushed to the ends of her hair and thanked the woman for her patience when she helped her in and out of the tub.

By the time Dr. Fabrizio pronounced her "healing nicely," Quinn was feeling a lot better. Her shoulder was tender and still needed to remain immobile, but the worst of her bruises and scrapes were fading. She switched to an over-the-counter painkiller, which meant she was more alert and she was permitted one short glass of wine with dinner.

Thus, she felt confident saying, "I can take a train to Vienna," when Micah's housekeeper was dispatched to pack her new clothes into her new luggage. Granted, that would all be tricky to manage on her own, but Micah was flying to Berlin. "Berlin is completely out of my way." And would keep her in his.

"We have the awards banquet." He glanced up from sliding his laptop into his leather bag. "If you think you're up for traveling alone to Vienna, you should be able to sit through a dinner and a handful of speeches—which will sap my strength, I'll grant you."

He was looking ridiculously gorgeous as usual. His crisp bone-colored trousers held a break over his Italian loafers. The sleeves of a matching pullover were draped over his pale blue shirt and tied beneath his open collar. The front spikes of his hair were bent under the weight of his sunglasses and his jaw was smooth from recently shaving.

"We'll stay the night in Berlin, then carry on to

Vienna tomorrow afternoon. Which reminds me, I'll want this hard drive if I'm working from there." He used his thumbprint to open a safe behind his desk.

"You're coming to Vienna? I thought you spent all your time in Berlin these days."

"We're building a new head office there so I've been on hand, but it's a quick flight if I'm needed. Why?" He paused to take in her reaction. "Would you prefer to be alone in Vienna?"

"It's your house, Micah. I'm not going to say when you can or can't stay in it. I just presumed we'd go our separate ways once I left here." She examined a hangnail.

He came to the front of his desk and leaned his hips there, arms folded as he regarded her. "I presumed we'd spend the next few weeks seeing where this relationship takes us."

Alarm leaped through her blood.

"We don't have a relationship. We can't. You live here, I live seven thousand kilometers that way." She thumbed over her shoulder without any sense of whether it was west or not.

"Let me say it differently," he said with flinty equanimity. "I would like to spend the next few weeks coming to a shared understanding of what this relationship is. For instance, this has been like old times, having you under my roof in the summer. Is that how you'd like it to remain?"

"With me freeloading off of you? I mean, sure, if that's what floats your boat."

"Don't do that, Quinn," he said very chillingly. "I give you what I'm comfortable giving. I wouldn't do it if I didn't want to. There's no obligation on your side, no catch, and no judgment on you for accepting."

"It's not a cup of coffee, Micah. These things are expensive." Even the laptop bag he'd given her, which he'd told her was pre-owned, was vintage Chanel. It was quilted denim with gold stitching and had a number of practical pockets within. She'd coveted it too much to refuse.

"They're just things," he dismissed.

"And that's all you're comfortable giving me?" She thought she was being very clever with that lofty remark, but as her gaze clashed with his, his eyes narrowed.

"Along with my time, yes, which I assure you I never waste. Are you prepared to give me yours?"

Her heart quivered in her chest. She did want more time with him. She had been dreading saying goodbye, thinking at least when he'd walked away from her in anger, she hadn't had to fight to keep her composure in front of him. It had been the proverbial bandage torn off without ceremony.

Spending weeks with him in Vienna would be a slow, painful peeling that would take some skin, she knew it would.

"Why does it bother you when I give you things?" he asked quietly. "I still remember all those clothes going back, you know. Why did you do that? Because

I had the temerity to point out you were too young for an affair with me?"

"No. Because—" He'd been furious over the nightclub debacle with Remy. She'd thought he blamed her for it. But yes, she had also been furious over his calling her a child.

It went even deeper than that, though.

"Because you don't have to take care of me." It was really hard to say that, given that he'd been taking really good care of her this week. She genuinely didn't know how she would have managed if he hadn't, but, "You're not the first to want to rescue me from my hard luck story, you know. That's why I don't tell it. I don't want to get used to this, Micah." Did he even realize the level of wealth and privilege he possessed? What a seduction it was for someone like her?

"My entire childhood was a parade of being given things that I started to care about only for them to get left behind as I was moved around. I can't let myself want things or care about them." The same went for people. "Everything disappears eventually. Nothing is permanent." No one was. Not Eden. Not him. "It's better when I end things on my own terms."

She would have crossed her arms if the one wasn't trapped in her padded sling. She used the other to press against the ache in her stomach.

"Use them while you're here, then. If you don't want to take them when you leave, then don't." He turned to zip his laptop bag, giving her the impression he would be deeply insulted if she returned everything again. Maybe even hurt.

When he turned back, his expression was bland. "But I'd like you to come to Berlin and the ceremony. Will you?"

Her mouth was too unsteady to form words. She nodded once, jerkily.

Because she wasn't ready to say goodbye yet.

Quinn had stayed in Micah's Greek villa, his château in Switzerland, his mansion in Paris and recently his lakeside villa in Bellagio. Flying in his private jet was also something she'd done, although this one was new.

"Smaller, faster and greener," he dismissed with a shrug.

It was still very sumptuous with its ivory-and-chrome decor. A curved sofa was tucked into a corner that otherwise hid the galley. A dining table between two comfortable chairs had the pattern of a chessboard inlaid upon its top. Abstract art and soft pillows added splashes of color and the crew was as courteous as ever.

All of that should have prepared her for his apartment in Berlin, but it was simply too modern and space-aged for her to keep her gasp of astonishment to herself.

Two walls of windows were slanted upward to a peak on the upper floor. A winding staircase made of chrome and glass slithered like quicksilver down to the main floor where the open concept was situated around a central fireplace. All the furnishings were sleek and contemporary and inviting. Outside on the terrace, an infinity pool glowed blue while the fading day turned the Berlin skyline mauve.

"I have some appointments. Ask Olga for anything you need." He had already introduced her to the housekeeper. "Your stylist will be here in two hours to help you get ready."

"My stylist? I thought this thing was for engineers and computer programmers. How formal is it? I only have what you've bought me so far." Terror was creeping in on her. She had thought the pleated skirt with a light jacket would be business-casual enough for the event.

"It's become quite splashy in recent years," he said with a fatalistic shrug. "The organizers began recognizing music video and cinema technologies alongside the architecture and automations so it garners more interest from the press. There will be a handful of celebrities presenting and accepting awards so there's a red carpet."

"And I have to walk it? With this?" She waved at the sling.

"Your stylist is bringing a selection of gowns. She knows your taste and your situation. I'm sure you'll find something that works. I have to run. I'll see you in a couple of hours." He touched a kiss to her slack lips and disappeared.

She panic-texted Eden, who called and did a poor job of relieving the sense of pressure.

"I think it's nice you two are going on a date."

"It's not a *date*," Quinn cried. "Why would you say that? Have you been talking to him about me?" She narrowed her eyes in suspicion.

"No. We texted about Mama's birthday the other day, but otherwise I've only been texting with you. What do you think tonight is, if not a date?"

"Bring Your Houseguest to Work Day," she cried, but her stylist arrived so they switched to Eden helping her choose a gown. They signed off when it was time for Quinn to have her hair and makeup done.

Quinn was not a girlie girl in the sense that Eden was, enjoying high fashion and cosmetics and complex hairstyles. Thankfully, her stylist did have a good sense of her tastes. She kept her makeup subtle and only set her hair so her wild curls fell in orderly ringlets. After that was done, she helped her into a strapless silk gown with a flattering princess cut that flared around her feet. A matching plum stole was a genius touch that allowed her to drape it around her upper arms and across her sling.

Nervously, she put on her shoes—pretty slingbacks that she was able to slip on easily—and carefully walked down the stairs, holding the rail and watching her step.

When she finally glanced up, she realized Micah had been standing below the whole time, watching her descend like a little fawn on its newborn legs.

She paused and clutched the rail tighter, feeling even weaker under the impact of his attention. It was such an intense blast, it nearly blew back her hair. It definitely left her heart tripping unsteadily. *He* did.

"I thought you were still in your room, changing." He was already in a tuxedo, freshly shaved and so flawless and casually sexy, she had to ask helplessly, "Why do you always look so good?"

His head went back slightly, as if the question didn't register.

"Probably because I wasn't allowed to leave my room unless I passed muster," he finally answered.

That took her aback. "What do you mean?"

"My grandmother was very fastidious about appearance. If she noticed one hair out of place, I was sent back upstairs. Sometimes that worked to my advantage. If I didn't want to go to a particular dinner or opera, I dripped some toothpaste on my shirt. Sometimes I missed something I wanted to attend, though. I learned to keep it tight."

"What kinds of things?" she asked with concern, recalling asking him if his father had been abusive. Apparently, the whole family was pretty heartless. "Birthday parties?"

"Science exhibits."

"Well, that's the cutest thing I've ever heard." She bit the inside of her lip to hide her amusement. "I often forget you're nothing but algorithms and loadspan calculations under those bespoke suits."

"And spreadsheets. I do love detailed analysis."

The way his gaze drifted over her told her exactly what kind of sheets he was referring to.

She blushed and chuckled, making herself finish descending the stairs, but her knees were not quite steady.

"You look beautiful," he said, gaze still drinking her in. "I mean, you're always beautiful, but—" He paused as she made a noise of skepticism. His brows rose imperiously. He came closer and tilted up her chin, forcing her to look him in the eye. "Strawberries and cream is my favorite dessert." His thumb caressed her cheek. "It doesn't have to be served in fine china for me to want to eat it, but when it is, I certainly appreciate the presentation."

She was trying to work up a snappy retort, but the housekeeper was bringing someone in from the foyer.

"Ah. This is Hans Gunter and he has something else I hope you'll wear. It's for a good cause," he assured her as Hans offered a large flat purple velvet box. "This necklace will be auctioned off in a few weeks to benefit an organization that helps children displaced by natural and man-made disasters."

The pendant was a cushion-cut purple amethyst surrounded by white-gold filigree with diamond accents. It came with a script about the auction. Apparently, Hans would shadow her throughout the evening to ensure its safety, but what was she going to do? Say no to helping children?

She turned and let Micah clasp the weighty stones around her neck.

A short while later, she was on Micah's arm, walking the red carpet, overwhelmed by all the shouting and camera flashes.

A microphone was shoved in her face and a vaguely familiar celebrity asked her, "Who are you wearing tonight?"

"The gown is from House of Lakshmi, the necklace is from the Barsi group. The sling is by prescription," she deadpanned.

That caused a ripple of laughter in the gallery and another flurry of flashes, but she and Micah were finally allowed to enter the building. The rest of the evening was sedate by comparison. Micah had ensured that everyone at their table spoke English and one was the wife of his project manager who worked at the Canadian embassy here in Berlin, which was a thoughtful touch on his part.

They ate and awards were presented, then the lights changed and the orchestra switched to ballroom tunes.

"Shall we?" Micah held out a hand. "We missed our chance at Eden's wedding to Hunter."

Quinn was so shocked by his saying that, as if he'd been looking forward to dancing with her, she let him lead her into the growing crowd. Once there, she had to admit, "I don't really know how to do this." She felt awkward with her one arm fixed in the sling and his searching for her waist beneath it.

"Let me lead." He shifted them slightly so one side of her body was pressed closer to his, then he easily guided her through the steps.

With him, anything physical was easy. Natural. As though they were made to move together in coordination.

"Thank you for coming tonight," he said. "Everyone is completely charmed by you."

Charmed? That was laying it on thick, but a short while later, one of his executives subtly prodded for details of their relationship.

"I don't think I've ever seen him bring a date to one of these things. Usually it's his assistant or a VIP from elsewhere."

Quinn started to brush that off and insist she was "just a friend of his sister," but stopped herself. It felt demeaning toward him and maybe herself to pretend they meant nothing to each other. What *did* they mean to each other, though?

She couldn't speak for his feelings. Passion, obviously, but she was always throwing herself at him. The fact that he didn't take other lovers, or seem to date anyone else, was heartening, but he was a busy man. It didn't follow that he preferred her in some way.

He was decent enough not to lead anyone on, though. And kind enough to spend a night in hospital with her. He was generous, but possessed enough acuity to know she would rather use the cost of a necklace to help children than own such an extravagant piece herself. Not that he would buy it for her in the first place. They weren't *that* tight.

But they were close enough he knew how to make her laugh. He made her feel a lot of things.

Oh, dear. As she struggled to close her clutch over the pearlescent pink lipstick she had just refreshed, she blinked hot eyes, fearful she was falling in love with him. No. She had always loved him, of course, in the way of an adolescent crush and "my best friend's brother" way. She had always trusted him and admired him and found him deeply attractive.

Somewhere along the line, she had managed to convince herself that she could feel all those things and keep those feelings in safe little boxes that wouldn't swish and leak into each other and flood her up with other more dangerous emotions like yearning and insatiable hunger for his attention. Like an attachment that needed to see him and hear his voice and touch him every single day.

No, Quinn. No. Everything ends. Everything.

Disturbed, she returned to the ballroom where he asked if she wanted to dance again.

"Do you mind if we leave? I'm ready to give up custody of this necklace."

The bodyguard signed for it the moment they returned to Micah's apartment, then left them alone.

"Nightcap?"

"No." She was still shaken at how her emotions were running away with her. She was at war with herself, wanting to self-protect, but also thinking that if things were going to end between them sooner rather than later, she wanted to make the most of the time they had.

"Tired?"

"No. I— Will you come to my room?" she asked in a request that left her standing out on a narrow plank.

He went still, not playing dumb, only saying solemnly, "I thought we weren't going to do that."

"I don't want to find words." There weren't any, not for all the emotions swirling in her. They were too vast and disarming. "I just want you."

Even saying that much left her walking a tightrope suspended between skyscrapers.

He ambled closer, exuding intensity and sexual tension. Gravity. His light touch on her jaw was almost electric, making her want to jolt away from a sting that wasn't there. At the same time, she wanted to fold in closer to him. She wanted his arms around her, sheltering her.

"Do I need a condom?"

"Not on my..." She cleared her throat, staring at the ruffles of his shirt. "I haven't been with anyone else."

"That means something, you know." His hand cupped the side of her neck, hot and heavy. He waited for her gaze to slowly climb to his. "We've seen each other nine times in four years and never slept with anyone else."

"You keep count?" He could probably feel her carotid artery pounding with her elevated pulse against the heel of his palm.

"You don't?"

Of course she did.

His thumb grazed her jaw. "I keep count of what counts, Quinn."

It's just sex, she wanted to argue, but she wasn't capable of just sex. She was realizing that as he dipped his head and brushed a soft kiss across her lips, once.

"Come to my room," he said in a low rumble.

"Why?"

"Because I want you in my bed." He took her hand and drew her up the stairs.

Her eyes were stinging. So was her throat. This was silly. They'd done this before. She wanted to make love with him. There was no reason to feel nervous, but she was suddenly clinging tightly to his hand so she wouldn't slip on the stairs. So she wouldn't slip up and let her heart show.

His room was the top of the spaceship, the walls and ceiling made of angled windows. The space was enormous, accommodating a massive bed and full sitting area. Toward the back, the shower was a huge cubicle in the middle of the room. One side was tiled and plumbed, the other open to the sunlight that would soak down from the windows. A freestanding tub stood nearby, close to the doors to the private terrace. The double doors to a walk-in closet were open; the single closed door likely led to the toilet.

He touched something on the wall and panels inside all of the glass panes began to lower, enclosing them in privacy.

It's an intriguing place to visit, but this is not your world, she reminded herself wistfully as she began to draw her stole free from its tuck against her sling.

Micah made a noise of protest. "Let me. I've been mentally undressing you all night."

She gave him an admonishing look as he carefully tugged the silk, slithering it across her bare shoulders in a way that caused her skin to roughen with goose bumps and her nipples to rise against the cups of her strapless bra.

"Don't worry. I admired other things about you." He sent the swatch of silk drifting toward a chair and moved behind her.

"Such as?" she prompted, cringing slightly that she was reduced to fishing for compliments.

"How easily you make people laugh." His fingers tickled her spine and her gown began to release. "I've always been envious of that."

Envious? It was a defense mechanism she had developed to avoid being picked on. He didn't need tricks like that because he had all of this.

He also had wide hands that slid into her open gown and caressed her waist and hips, making her stomach muscles quiver while her brain blanked.

Cool silk brushed her thighs as it fell, but he didn't let her step out of it. He stayed behind her, roaming his light touch across her skin, finding the lace of her silver bra and matching cheekies. His touch seemed a random map until she realized each pause of his touch was extra sensitive because he was trying to erase her bruises with the brush of his fingertip.

"Are you sure you're up for this?" he murmured.

"Yes." She was already shaking with anticipation. Surely he could see that.

"I'll be careful with you," he promised in a voice that rasped across her senses. He set his mouth against her nape, hot enough to brand her skin.

She lifted her hand, wanting to touch him, but she could only sift her fingertips through his hair as he placed more of those tender kisses across her shoulders and spine.

She had missed him, missed touching him. Being naked and close and awash in the kind of pleasure that erased all the pain of living.

His mouth opened and he scraped his teeth on the taut tendon in her neck, making her gasp.

"I like that," he said, wrapping his arm around her stomach to draw her back into the rough-soft textures of his tuxedo. "I live for the way we react to each other."

"Be careful of the gown," she said, aware of it piled around their shoes, but he slid his hand into the front of her underpants and she lost her voice.

She held still, afraid of trampling the gown, erotically trapped in the cage of his arms. Trapped between the wall of his clothed body and the blatant caress of his fingertip teasing her lips apart, seeking moisture and spreading it. As he lazily tantalized the knot of nerves, she shivered and turned her head, searching for his mouth.

He only teased her with a kiss on her cheek and the corner of her lips. "Tell me what you want," he said in that wicked grate of a voice. "Tell me when you're close."

"I am," she moaned, lifting her hips into his touch, then rocking back to grind into the erection prodding through his trousers at her backside. "Harder. Don't stop," she pleaded.

His arm around her shifted. He avoided her sling and slid his touch to cup her breast. While his thumb pressed her nipple through her bra, his other hand continued to circle and delicately torture her until she lost her ability to breathe. Lovely shudders washed over her, weakening her knees.

He held her in strong arms, mouth pinned to her neck where he left a sting and a rueful curse a moment later.

"I've just added to your bruises." He kissed the damp spot. "I thought I was going over with you."

She was dizzy and blinking herself back to reality, barely tracking as he released her bra and dropped her underwear, then guided her to the bed where he sat her on the edge to remove her shoes.

He stayed there on his knees while he kissed her a long time, until she was clinging her good arm around his shoulders and nearly off the bed and into his lap, she was so eager to be close to him. She wanted the hair of his chest on her breasts, the hot shape of his sex against her mound. She wanted their mouths sealed and their legs intertwined.

She couldn't touch enough of him, couldn't get close enough, darn this wretched sling!

"Don't do that," he admonished, misconstruing her noise of anguish. "I said I'd be careful with you and I will." He nuzzled against the strap of her sling where it sat above her breast, then flashed her a look of lusty amusement. "I kind of like this bondage situation that forces you to be still while I have my way with you."

"It turns you on?" She tried to sound disparaging, but wicked excitement tightened her nipples and sent a fresh wash of heat into the juncture of her thighs.

"It really does." He reached for a couple of pillows and stacked them behind her, urging her to recline on them while he stayed on the floor and ran his free hand over her stomach and thighs, then up to her breast. He cupped one and leaned to give her nipple a lascivious lick. "I'm going to kiss every inch of you and you're going to lie there and take it."

For some reason, that scared the hell out of her. Not that she felt genuinely helpless. She knew he would stop if she told him to, but the way he picked up her hand and set his lips on the inside of her wrist, then trailed kisses to her elbow made her shake. It was too tender. Too sweet. It made her feel special and cherished and she *wasn't*.

But she wanted to be. She wanted this shower of

care and attention. She drank it in like a desert cactus soaked up rain after a hundred years' drought.

"Micah." She tried to caress his erection and tease him into the same blind lust that was gripping her, but he shifted, leaving her breasts and collarbone for the tremulous territory of her navel. "I really want you inside me."

"I want that, too." He nipped the point of her hip. "I can't wait to feel you gripping and shattering around me. But look how pretty you are." His one hand plumped her breast and he rose to suck her nipple again.

Lightning shot between her legs. She tried to press her thighs together, but he was in the way. There was no relief.

He sent her a knowing look and dipped a little lower, touching his mouth to her loosely curled hand where it stuck out of the sling. His tongue prodded at the seam of her fingers, right below her knuckle, and another wave of heat washed through her.

"You're being…" She couldn't think words.

"Thorough?" He moved to touch kisses all across her quivering abdomen, then rubbed one side of his face and the other like a giant cat who seemed to be affectionate, but was actually leaving his scent on her skin. Such a possessive male.

With casual strength, he lifted her knee, tipping her more fully into the pillows behind her as he parted her legs so he could kiss the inside of one thigh.

She had never felt so much his. *Claimed.* Her loins

pulsed with longing, but he teased his attention all the way down her calf before kissing and caressing his way up her other leg, driving her mad with want.

Only when her legs were shaking and she thought she would die if he didn't penetrate her did he hiss in a breath of tested control. He left her weak and sprawled on the pillows while he rose to shed his own clothes without ceremony, revealing his muscled chest and the hair bisecting his tense abdomen. The pale skin behind his boxer briefs appeared along with the steely thrust of his erection.

"I could—"

"I would kill for that, I really would, but I need to be inside you, Quinn." He slid onto the bed and drew a pillow close, inviting her to spoon in front of him so her injured shoulder could sit on the pillow, elevated and protected.

"I want to touch you," she sobbed even as she maneuvered into a position that should have felt awkward, but was actually really comfortable.

"Poor you," he crooned without any mercy whatsoever. "I get to touch you however I want." He slid his splayed hand across her hip and down her thigh, adjusting her leg as he settled closer in behind her. Then he guided his tip between her thighs, searching out her aching core. "This is how I want you to hold me. When you're tight around me, I think I'm going to die from how good it feels."

"Yes." Her voice throbbed. "Do it."

A rough noise escaped him and he shifted slightly, gaining leverage to press inside her.

She tried to hold herself still for him, but she was shaking with arousal. Utterly boneless and weak with wanting.

Rising on his elbow behind her, he surged his hips against her backside. She arched, trying to accept more of his thick, hot presence within her. She wanted it fast and hard, but this position left all the power up to him.

"Softly," he whispered against her cheek. "You know I'll wait for you. Relax and let me make it good for you."

He was talking about an orgasm, but his words went straight into her heart, past all her firmest defenses. Tears of yearning sprang to the backs of her eyes so she had to close them tight. It was her only way to hide, but there was no hiding from the exquisite sensation of his flesh dragging and resurging into her. He moved with gentle, lazy power, sending wave after wave of joy through her. He was generous and patient and determined to draw out their pleasure as much as possible.

"Micah!" She clenched her hand in the blanket, feeling as though he was breaking her apart, it was so unbearably good.

"You're so perfect, Quinn," he was crooning, hand playing across her stomach and thighs like a violin with a bow. "How do we ever walk away from this?"

She couldn't answer. She was submerged in a sea

of pleasure, rocked by his easy thrusts. His whole body was tense and shaking with the control he was exerting, but he held himself from crushing her as he held himself back from the wild tempo they usually sought.

He held them on the precipice of absolute perfection.

With no other way to express her tortured joy, she groaned out her pleasure.

"I need you," she moaned. "I need you so much." It hurt to say it. To know it was true. To *feel* it. If she wasn't careful, she would give him every last shred of herself.

"I've got you," he murmured, and his touch moved to where she was clamping her slick flesh upon him. He caressed her and suddenly the climax that had been soaring and circling out of reach plunged down like a raptor, swooping and pulling a sharp cry from her lips.

As she tumbled off the cliff, awash in powerful contractions, he pinned his hips to her backside, set his teeth on her earlobe, and released the longest, sexiest groan in history.

CHAPTER TEN

Micah had already made up his mind to ask Quinn to marry him before they arrived in Berlin. Waking beside her every day for a week had only reinforced his decision, but he waited for the rings to be sized and catch up to them in Vienna.

This apartment was one of his smaller properties, but also one of his favorites. Built in the 1860s for an industrialist, the exterior melded with Vienna's rich history. The handful of units within were spacious and updated for modern life while Old World touches remained, like parquet flooring and a wine-making operation beneath street level.

When his housekeeper pointed out the courier parcel that had been brought up first thing, he ordered bubbly from his private reserves in the cellar. It went into a bucket next to the breakfast table.

He could have waited until dinner, but twice this week, Quinn had been so caught up in research, she had stayed late. Other times, he heard her through the door between their offices, dictating notes and stumbling into the occasional trouble with them.

"Scratch that. Scratch that. Don't type *scratch that* you idiotic—stop! End! Quit document you absolute—ahh! *Stop.*"

After a late night, however, they'd agreed to have a lazy start today. He was sipping his coffee, reading headlines on his tablet, when she came down the stairs.

She had managed to knot a scarf around the loose corkscrews of her hair and had dressed in wide-legged pants with one of the sleeveless wrap tops she seemed to find so convenient to put on and take off.

"Hungry?" he asked.

"Don't be smug." She was still yawning and blinking, but gave him a smug smile of her own. She was feeling much better these days and last night had been a taste of their previous energetic and adventurous encounters.

"I damned well will be. For once, I left you sleeping. Come here."

She wrinkled her nose at him, but bypassed her own chair to come give him a kiss that tasted of toothpaste.

He resisted the urge to pull her into his lap. Barely. Especially when his gaze found her modest cleavage before she straightened. Those freckles sprinkled across the upper swells of her breasts never ceased to mesmerize him.

"Where are we going today?" she asked as she moved to her chair.

"I thought we decided to walk in the park." He deliberately didn't rise to help her. She was already sinking into it and he was waiting for her to notice what was on her plate.

"Maybe we could visit the—" She cut herself off and stared at the green velvet box. It was open, showing a set of three rings. The two wedding bands were almost identical. His was a wider band of gold, but they both held a stripe of flush-mounted diamonds across the top. The engagement ring was similar, but it held a break where a large square-cut diamond floated, also flush with the rest of the setting so it wouldn't catch easily.

It was clever and understated in its artistry, both beautiful and complex, if one took the time to notice. Like her.

"Before you make a crack about getting your minerals…" Had she gone pale? An uncharacteristic jab of self-doubt shot through him. "I propose we marry."

She closed the box with a snap and set it aside, hand shaking. "Would you pour me a coffee, please?"

Wow. He genuinely felt like he'd been kicked in the face.

He poured, brain going numb. He nodded as the housekeeper peeked in. Seconds later, she brought in the serving dishes filled with a ham and potato

hash, eggs in mustard sauce, and an oven-baked pan-
cake sprinkled with powdered sugar and fresh fruit.

"Is that your answer?" he asked when his housekeeper had retreated.

"You already know my answer, Micah. I don't
believe in marriage."

"Marriage isn't like Santa Claus. It's not something made up by—"

"The church?" she cut in crisply.

"It's a commitment, not a human rights violation.
I won't keep you from having a career, if that's what
you're afraid of. Finish your doctorate. I'll support
you in every way I can."

"Then what? You'll move to Canada so I can work
there?"

He had never seen her as a naive person. "Brace
yourself for a hard truth, Quinn. As admirable as it
is that you want to bring about change in government
policy, that's not where true power lies. Use me. Use
my wealth and position to get the results you want."

Dismay and conflict flexed through her expression. "Become part of what's most wrong in this
world? Is that why you want to marry me? To keep
me from challenging the order that benefits you so
much?"

"No," he said flatly, biting back a curse. "It's not
that complicated. I want to marry you so I can wake
up next to you every morning." Most mornings it was
a very pleasant start to his day.

"That is not what you want," she returned hotly,

voice turning strident with anxiety. "I know that your aunt is after you to marry and secure the family legacy. Eden told me that ages ago. I'm not going to give you babies, Micah. *Ever.*"

"I didn't ask you to." He tried not to shorten his tone, but rejection was not something he suffered often. It stung, especially from her. Like this. She wasn't even considering it. "Although I am compelled to point out there are arrangements like surrogacy."

"It's not just about carrying a pregnancy."

"What then? Because I would love to understand your aversion. I would think someone without family would want to make one of her own."

She flashed him a look, one brimming with umbrage at not being understood before her brow flinched. She looked past him, mouth briefly working to find words.

"I do think about children sometimes, but I can't get past..." She stabbed a bite of egg, but left it on her fork, staring at it sickly. "What if I die? Then I've left a child to navigate this world alone, the same as I've had to."

His heart flipped over. "Don't say that. You're healthy."

"I was hit by a bicycle. It could have been a car. Life is tenuous."

"Nevertheless, Eden would—"

"I would never ask her to raise my child," she cut

in with aversion. "She wants to start her own family with Remy."

"Exactly. She's not afraid of what *might* happen. She's getting on with the business of living."

"And good for her! But they have a wide network of people who would race in to take their baby if something happened to them. I don't have that, Micah. Even if I adopted a child, I would still be running a risk of leaving them with nothing and no one."

"What about me? I have family."

"The family who persecuted your mother into abandoning you? The people who already think I'm not good enough for you? The ones who ostracized you when you misbuttoned your shirt? Those are the people you want raising your child?"

He pressed his lips together, not answering, but she was right. He wouldn't want his child raised by anyone with the last name Gould. Maybe not even himself. Micah viewed his role in this family as a gatekeeper who stopped them from spiraling back into the avarice that had been his father's trademark, but he was always on guard against selfish behaviors of his own.

As for his mother, as much as she would want to raise his child, the stark truth was that she was aging and still grieving the loss of Eden's father. Micah wasn't inclined to write off Eden as quickly as Quinn did, but his sister *would* be having her own children soon. And, as much as Eden's father had welcomed Micah as if he was his own son, the knowledge that

Micah wasn't really part of his mother's second family had always been blindingly obvious to him.

"I'm sorry if staying here with you has led you to think I would want this," Quinn said shakily. "I'll—"

"Do not say you are going back to Canada. You are not running away. You want to know why I want to marry you? So you'll have to sit there and work things out with me for a change."

"There's nothing to work out," Quinn insisted, and did walk away.

Quinn's heart was knocked sideways by his proposal. On the one hand, it suggested he had deeper feelings for her than he'd ever let on, but it also felt threatening.

She had promised herself for years that she would never marry. Partly because, as a feminist, she did think marriage was an outdated institution, but, more importantly, as someone who had been dependent on people who didn't really care about her, she couldn't stomach anything but complete self-sufficiency.

That was why she had made such a point of keeping an ocean and every other type of boundary between herself and Micah. At least, she had managed to until this last week when she had become almost completely reliant on him.

Even on an emotional level, she was sliding down a slippery slope.

She further panicked when she arrived in the room they shared. The bed was still mussed from their active night, reminding her of all she would be giving up if she ran away, but she genuinely felt herself in peril. If she stayed, she would finish falling in love with him. Her heartbreak would be even greater when everything fell apart later so why not leave now, when it was on her terms?

Amid her agitated flitting, trying to work out what to do, her phone pinged with a text.

Yasmine.

Can you call me when you have a minute? Any time is fine.

Worried it had something to do with Remy and therefore Eden, Quinn jabbed the button for a video chat.

"That was fast. Hi! How *are* you?" Yasmine greeted brightly. She wore a colorful scarf over her locks, shimmery gold eyeshadow and violet lipstick. "Remy told me about your shoulder. I thought if you're in a sling, you wouldn't want to type."

"Calling is easier. Thanks." Her heart warmed that Yasmine was so understanding. "So this is a social call? I was worried something was wrong."

"No, I'm fine. Definitely social." A pause, then, "Mostly."

"Oh? Do you need something?"

"No," she insisted. "No, I actually saw your photo on the red carpet in Berlin and I guess I was surprised you were still, um…" Her gaze seemed to search Quinn's through the screen. "Seeing Micah."

"I'm not." Her own voice sounded so high she thought it ought to crack the screen on her phone. "I've been staying with him, but I was thinking about checking flights to Canada today—"

She realized Micah had come to the bedroom door.

She swallowed as she met his grim expression.

"I heard my name. Is that Eden?"

"Yasmine." Her throat dried to a rasp.

His cheek ticked once before he drew the door shut and, presumably, walked back downstairs. Maybe left the apartment and the building and the country.

Oh God.

"Is it bad that we're talking? I didn't mean to start anything between you," Yasmine moaned.

"You didn't. I promise. We're going through our own thing."

"Oh?" That was concern, not lurid curiosity, but Quinn didn't want to get into her own baggage about marriage and family and how very deeply she was hung up on Micah.

"It's nothing. Honestly," Quinn lied.

"How, um… How is he?" Yasmine asked apprehensively. "Remy told me he knows about me. Is that why he walked away? Believe me, I get that he needs time. I wasn't trying to impose myself on him. Oh, maybe I was trying to get his temperature," she acknowledged with a small cringe.

"It's understandable that you're curious," Quinn said faintly.

"I am, but..." She blew out a breath. "Eden mentioned introducing us when he comes to Canada for their mother's birthday. I don't want to put him on the spot like that. And with Remy there, weighing everything we might say to each other? That would be way too much tension for everyone involved. I guess I called you hoping you would tell him I don't expect him to meet me if he doesn't want to."

"I can do that," Quinn promised.

"But if he does want to meet, I would like that," she hurried to say, brow crinkled with distress. "I shouldn't put this on you. Honestly, when I realized you were still in Europe, my first thought was to ask if you want to get coffee sometime. I'm in Paris for a few weeks. Now I feel like I've dumped all over you. I'm sorry."

"Don't apologize! I want to help if I can." Quinn lowered onto the edge of the bed, never wanting to be the one in need, but always a sucker for being needed. "I don't want to speak for Micah or how he feels, but I'll definitely tell him what you've told me. And I would love to get coffee. With or without him."

"Thank you. I would love that."

"I'll get in touch once I've figured some things out."

"Thank you."

* * *

She was going to check flights?

Micah didn't know who he was angrier with, Quinn or himself. He should have broached marriage as a discussion, not presented her with the rings. He knew she didn't like people making decisions for her. He had thought it would be a romantic surprise, but now he wanted to throw the damned things out the window.

And she was up there talking to Yasmine? About him? He would never tell her who she could be friends with, but that was a slap in the face, it really was.

Not that he could avoid the reality of his secret half sister forever. He had shoved her into a file labeled "later" because it was too hard to look at. Micah's father had been a master of dirty deals, building his fortune on exploited workers and intimidation tactics. He had deliberately taunted Lucille with her access to Micah, using him to punish her for leaving.

Then he'd lost his memory to all of that, succumbing to early onset dementia just as Micah was growing into a full awareness of his father's character flaws.

Only nineteen and not even finished school, his father's allies had thought they could turn Micah into their puppet and pressed him to step into his father's shoes.

Micah hadn't wanted to assume such a soiled heritage, but it was the only way to clean it. The moment he'd been given the seat at the head of the table, he'd begun what was now referred to as the Great Purge. He'd fired backstabbing cronies and put people like his aunt on notice. He had made clear they could follow him into the new way of doing things—with ethics and transparency—or strike out on their own.

Once everyone understood that he wielded power rather than being seduced by it, they began coming onto his side.

He probably would have fallen in with the old, corrupt ways if he hadn't had his mother's influence and—even more so—his sister's. Lucille refused to come to Europe, but Eden had been Micah's semiannual reward for wading through the muck. He would send for her on school holidays and her spritely energy would remind him there was good in the world. And that it was up to people like him to make sure people like her didn't become cynical and disillusioned.

Then there was Quinn. Had she influenced him? Absolutely. Some of Eden's friends had been the sort of opportunists he was all too familiar with. He'd vetted them and discouraged her from pursuing those friendships, but Quinn had been so ethically solid, she was almost annoying with it. Did she put him on notice every single time he slipped toward patriarchal attitudes? Hell, yes.

She had pushed him to be better. To walk the walk. Slowly, Micah had evolved into a man who was still jaded and cautious, but one who was honest and fair. He might have gone so far as to call himself honorable.

He had believed he had made up for his father's worst transgressions.

Then he learned of Yasmine. She was proof that his father had sunk even lower than Micah could have imagined. How could he not feel the rot of it all over him?

How could he expect Quinn to attach herself to that? Was that the real source of her refusal to marry him?

"Micah?"

He stiffened and tried to curl his hand into a fist in his pocket, but the ring box prevented it. He turned.

She chewed the corner of her lip.

"Yes?" he prompted. If she was leaving, he wanted her to say it, not stand there blinking at him like she had a grim medical diagnosis to impart.

"Yasmine is in Paris. She asked me if I wanted to meet up with her. The invitation includes you."

He snapped his head back, not expecting that.

"There's no obligation," she assured him.

"But you'll meet with her regardless." His sternum turned to rusty iron. He looked to the window again.

"Not necessarily. I wanted to see where your thoughts were." She edged closer, brow pulled with consternation. "She said Eden mentioned introducing you two when you go for Lucille's birthday."

Micah choked out a curse, not ready to participate in *that* family dinner. He loved Eden, he really did, but she was such a glass half-full. If he didn't run through a meadow and catch his long-lost sister in his arms, Eden would be devastated.

"Yasmine thought that was a lot to put on both of you." Quinn's voice was rueful. She knew exactly where Eden's best qualities tipped toward impossible to live up to. She touched his sleeve. "It's completely up to you, but I have to wonder if the prospect of meeting her will hang over both your heads until it's done. I could go with you," she offered gently.

"To Paris?"

"Or somewhere else. What's halfway between Vienna and— Oh. Switzerland." She lifted her brows in discovery. "The great bastion of neutrality."

He twisted his mouth, but he didn't hate the idea. At least it would give him something different to brood about that wasn't Quinn.

"Yes." Even as he nodded, his mind skipped ahead to all the arrangements he'd been contemplating where Yasmine was concerned. "Set it up."

CHAPTER ELEVEN

QUINN FEARED SHE was prodding Micah onto a plank of some kind.

He became very remote as she and Yasmine took a few days to firm things up. He left for meetings and accepted calls at odd hours and, even though they continued to sleep together, he came to bed late and rose before she woke. He asked about her museum research a couple of times, but she could tell he was only half listening.

Desperate to reach him in some small way, she joined him in the shower the morning they were heading to Zurich. She was allowed to remove her sling for bathing now and had begun some rehabilitation exercises, mostly to ensure the rest of her arm didn't atrophy while her shoulder finished healing.

His whole body went tense as he raked his gaze down her naked form, but he waited until she touched him, pressing her cool body up against his hot, wet one. Then he fell on her like a starving wolf, consuming her lips and pressing her to the tiled wall before he dropped to his knees and pleasured her with his mouth.

She was still weak and dazed from a powerful climax when she realized he was using his fist to take care of his own orgasm, groaning into the spray as he did so.

"Micah." She tried to catch at his shoulder.

"Thank you for that, but—" He cupped her cheek and pressed one hard, wet kiss across her mouth. His eyes didn't meet hers. He looked to be in pain of some sort, but he only said, "We should get on the road. Traffic might be heavy this morning."

With a huff of disbelief, she finished showering alone.

Doubts were firmly entrenched in her by the time they landed in Zurich. Yasmine had suggested a picturesque village not far from the city. It only had cable cars, no real ones. One would carry them up the mountain to a restaurant built into the cliffs.

It had sounded like a pleasant setting that would give them something to talk about so they wouldn't feel pressured to dig through difficult emotions, but Micah had become the most aloof, impossible-to-read version of himself.

Quinn feared Yasmine would take that as dislike or rebuff. Her own palms were sweating, but as the cable car gently swayed on its way up the mountainside, she reached to hold his hand.

For a moment, he didn't react to her touch on the

back of his. Then he turned his head to ask distantly, "Why did you come?"

"What do you mean? I said I would."

"But why? To see Yasmine?"

A small sob of helplessness left her. "Why did you come to the hospital even though we'd had a huge fight?"

He grumbled out a noise, but his hand turned to grasp hers. He didn't let go as they took the short walk from the cable car terminus to the restaurant.

Yasmine was seated under a big red patio umbrella on the terrace. She waved and stood, smiling nervously. Her outfit was vaguely safari inspired, but turquoise with bright yellow palm fronds painted across the fabric. Her makeup was toned down from her usual, but still shimmery and colorful.

"This place is amazing," Quinn said as they briefly embraced. "I'm so glad you recommended it."

"I didn't know how to dress. Am I going for lunch? Are we hiking?" Yasmine turned her heavy boot, then thrust out her hand to Micah. It was visibly trembling. Her dark brown eyes were wary, yet seeking. "Hi. I'm Yasmine."

Quinn held her breath.

"Micah." He took her hand and shook it. Gently. His voice wasn't quite steady and some of his frost melted away so fast, he seemed to flinch at the sting. "It's good to meet you."

In that moment, Quinn knew she was in love with

him. Completely, utterly, "tumble all the way to the bottom of the valley" in love.

Micah couldn't have done this without Quinn here.

She made Yasmine laugh and kept the conversation moving. Occasionally, Yasmine asked him a direct question, mostly innocuous things about travel and whether his company did this or that. Twice she uncannily did exactly as he did, once by ordering the same sandwich without cheese—sacrilege in this corner of the world, but like him, she didn't care for it. Then, after lunch, she chose the same hiking trail he preferred.

Granted, there were only three to choose from, but Quinn wanted to go down to the alpine lake.

"Then we have to walk back up," Micah and Yasmine said at the same time.

"I'll go as far as that lookout and take a photo. You two go ahead. I'll catch up."

"Subtle," Micah said as Quinn darted down the path. He resisted the urge to call out that she should hold the rail. She wasn't a child, but he'd be damned if he would let her put herself back in hospital.

"I like her a lot," Yasmine said as they began to stroll along the trail.

"I don't know anyone who doesn't." Except herself, Micah realized with a jolt. Not that Quinn hated herself. She wasn't that twisted, but he didn't think she appreciated how special she was.

"Thank you for coming," Yasmine said with an

earnest flash in her gaze. "I know it must have been hard news to hear."

"That my father was a monster? It wasn't news to me that he was one, only the full extent." He paused at a rail that allowed him to see Quinn below, taking photos of the sharp peaks across the valley. "I'm sorry, Yasmine. I'm truly sorry for what he put your mother through. Your whole family. And for how I've behaved at different times, believing my father's version of the past."

"There was no one to tell you differently. My parents hid the truth even from me." Her smile flickered and faltered. "To be fair, my father did actually double-cross yours."

In retaliation for the crime against his wife. Micah didn't blame him for that, especially when Kelvin Gould had made every effort to punish them. Her parents had had to move to Canada to get away from his father's attempts to destroy them financially.

"I want you to know that I've spent the last few days asking my legal and accounting teams for a market value assessment of all that I inherited from my father."

"Oh my God. Micah, no. That's not why I wanted to meet you." She was horrified.

He wasn't surprised by her refusal, but ignored it.

"I know it won't make things right, but it's important to me to try. Your parents might be gone, but your family deserves compensation for what my father put them through. They would have had a different life if my father hadn't made it impossible for them to stay in Paris. And you have certain claims that are rightfully yours. A board seat. We can find a way to appoint someone to vote your share if you don't want to identify yourself to the rest of my family. I completely understand if you would rather not. At some point I'll have to tell them that my father was responsible for another child. They'll want a paternity test, but we can redact your name and all of that can wait until you and I have negotiated the settlement."

"Micah, *please*." Her eyes were boggled. "All of my needs are met. I don't need anything from you."

"It's not from me, Yasmine. It's what he should have done. Don't let him get away with what he did. Don't let the rest of his family blindly continue to benefit from his lack of consequence."

She frowned with consternation, absorbing that.

Quinn finally caught up to them. She was clutching her chest, huffing and puffing. "I forgot about the elevation. That climb nearly killed me."

"We didn't want to be right," Yasmine said, following as Micah steered Quinn toward a nearby bench.

"It just comes naturally?" Quinn suggested pithily, looking between them.

Micah shared a smirk with his sister.

Micah seemed both relaxed yet still keyed up as they returned to Vienna late the next day.

By then, they had sent a group selfie to Eden who had soon replied.

This makes me so happy! It's my new lock screen.

Privately, Eden had messaged Quinn.

When are you going to tell me what's going on between you and Micah?

"Why am I here and not on my yacht?" Micah asked as they started to take a glass of wine onto the terrace only to be chased back inside by the dry city heat.

"Don't let me hold you back." Now that the visit with Yasmine was out of the way, the argument they'd had the morning over the rings seemed to flood back in and fill the room.

"You need to know something." Micah eyed her over the rim of his glass as he took a healthy gulp.

"What?" She froze part way to seating herself on the sofa.

"I've made a decision." He moved to top up his glass. "I'm not going to make children, either."

"What—? That's a pretty big decision, especially for a man in your position. And there's no danger for you, physically. Unless you're concerned something of your father would be replicated in your child? You and Yasmine both turned out to be kind, upstanding human beings. I think his behavior was more nurture than nature. Don't feel like you have to nip off your branch. I don't think it's diseased."

"I'm not suggesting that. Yasmine can have all the kids she wants and they can inherit an appropriate share of the company. That's fair and right. But I told her she shouldn't let my family benefit from the fact that my father never suffered the consequences of his actions. I meant it. If my aunt wants so badly to see her brother's bloodline continue, she can ask Yasmine very nicely if she's willing to do so, but I won't produce children for the sole purpose of ensuring his DNA maintains possession of all he acquired. That's wrong."

"You could have children because you want them," she pointed out. "And they just happen to inherit all this. You feel one way now, but you don't know how you'll feel in the future."

"Excuse me, Quinn," he said with heavy irony. "But are you trying to say I'm not capable of knowing my own mind and making my own decisions around reproduction?"

She bit her lip, chastised, but amused. "You know I hate it when you throw my own words back at me."

"That's why I do it." He took another generous swallow from his frosted glass. "It's not as impulsive as it sounds. The pressure from my aunt has always bothered me, probably because you've drilled into me what an archaic system progeniture is. My own father didn't want to be a father. He accidentally got my mother pregnant and married her because his

mother said she might be carrying his potential heir.
Potential. If I'd been a girl, there would have been a
quiet divorce and she would have been raised in Canada with a lot less baggage to carry around and none
of the responsibility I shoulder. Then, because I was
his heir, my father used that fact to push my mother
out of my life. She wasn't deemed good enough to
'prepare' me for this life. Can you imagine what sort
of sociopath I would be if I hadn't had her and Eden?
So no. I refuse to make children knowing they would
have to bear the weight of these same expectations."

She watched him pace a few steps, not knowing
what to say.

"Having said that…" He paused and looked
straight at her. "If you wanted to foster or adopt,
I'd be open to it. I think you'd make an incredible
mother. I don't know what kind of father I'd make,
though. Better than my own, I would hope." His brow
furrowed in contemplation.

Her heart melted into a puddle inside her chest.
She opened her mouth, but still couldn't find words.
Her eyes were blurring.

A week ago, he had proposed and she had thrown
up a wall of defensiveness, terrified at the prospect.
Now she knew herself deeply in love with him. If
she hadn't been, this little speech of his would have
done it.

"Micah, why did you offer me those rings?"

She didn't expect him to say he loved her, but

maybe she hoped he would. Maybe that's why she was holding her breath.

His expression grew somber. He sat down and set aside his glass, letting his hands hang loosely between his knees as he leaned forward with his elbows on his thighs.

"We're good together, Quinn. You know we are." He held her gaze with magnetic force. "I want to be together, every day. Otherwise, I'll be worried you're being run down by some other idiot who isn't paying attention. Is there some other man you're anxious to be with? Because I'm the one you keep coming back to. I want to make it official. That's all."

No words of love, then, but according to him, love was just something that looked pretty on a greeting card anyway.

She wanted to tell him that love was actually something that licked inside you like flames. It was a hungry fire that she knew would only smolder and make her feel acrid if she didn't see him every day to keep it bright and warm.

She couldn't say the words, though. She didn't want to see his pitiful look at her deluding herself that it existed.

She left her seat and let her knees touch the floor between his feet.

As he blinked in surprise, she cupped the side of his face. "Micah, will you marry me?"

His nostrils pinched as he drew in a sharp breath. His cheekbones seemed to stand out tautly. A dozen emotions flickered across his face, each gone faster than she was able to interpret, but the hot satisfaction at the end lingered. The tenderness that shone from his eyes bathed her in the sweetest, softest, warmest light.

"That scream you just heard was my sister starting to plan our wedding. C'mere." He gathered her into his lap and kissed her.

They spent two weeks on his yacht where Quinn diligently did her exercises and rehabilitated her arm with some lazy swimming. When they detoured through Bellagio on their way to Lucille's birthday in Canada, Quinn was pronounced by Dr. Fabrizio "better than new."

Micah breathed a sigh of relief, but he then had his mother's dinner to endure.

It began with an ecstatic Eden running out to embrace both of them, over the moon about their engagement.

Yasmine had been invited and waited on the porch with Remy and his mother. Lucille was equally teary and welcoming. Yasmine beamed widely and hugged them both.

Remy was far more circumspect. He nodded at Micah and greeted Quinn with what looked like genuine warmth. They all trailed inside where the women were soon chattering bridal showers, engagement parties and wedding plans.

"Just a wedding," Quinn insisted. She explained

that she had decided to put her PhD on hold. "There's an interesting opportunity at the Canadian embassy in Berlin that I've put in for. Even if I don't get that one, now that I see what might be available if I look, I'd rather work for a few years, then go back for my doctorate."

"Before the babies start coming," Lucille said brightly.

Micah stepped in before Quinn had to respond to that.

"Mom, would you consider coming to Germany for the wedding? It's a big ask, considering who will be there." He meant his family. "But the hotel renovations in Wildenfels are nearly complete. We could book it out before the official opening in October." The project was ahead of schedule and he and Quinn were planning to spend the next weeks in Berlin so the residency requirement would be easy to meet. "It's convenient for the business associates I'm expected to invite."

"It won't be a huge wedding anyway," Quinn interjected. "This is friends of the bride right here." She drew a circle to indicate their little party. "And you're all related to Micah."

"That's not true," Eden scoffed, and began rattling off mutual friends from school who absolutely *had* to be invited.

Quinn had floated the idea of an elopement, but since German marriages were typically conducted in private civil ceremonies at a registrar's office, and the pomp was actually the reception, she had agreed to Micah's desire for something bigger. He didn't want any rumors it was a shotgun wedding. A splashy celebration would set the appropriate tone, especially with his father's side of the family.

"I would go anywhere to see you two marry," Lucille assured them. "When were you thinking?"

"The hotel is scheduled to open in a month, so three weeks from today."

"That's not enough time!" Eden cried.

It was too long, in Micah's opinion.

"If I'm designing your gown, that starts today. Let me get my tablet," Yasmine said, searching for her bag.

"Mama, do you still have those bridal magazines from when I was planning my wedding to Hunter? They always have checklists in them." Eden turned on Micah. "I know what you're doing. You're making this happen fast so I don't have time to go over-the-top with the arrangements. You are underestimating me, my friend," Eden warned playfully.

Quinn, the devil, took advantage of the mild chaos to bring Micah two open longneck bottles of beer. She tilted her head toward Remy. He was pretending an interest in a romance novel Lucille had left on an end table.

"Take him outside and tell him about your dream wedding. Or discuss women's rights. Or socket wrenches. Dealer's choice."

He knew damned well what she wanted him to

talk to Remy about. He walked over to offer one of the bottles. "Shall we get this over with?"

Remy accepted the beer and nodded for Micah to precede him out to Lucille's extremely well-tended garden. She opened it for a week every summer to walking tours as part of a cancer research fundraiser so it was an immaculate network of paths among water features, a freestanding swing, and a "pollinator's paradise" of fragrant blooms that attracted butterflies and other insects.

"Congratulations on your engagement," Remy said, helping himself to a raspberry off a cane.

"Congratulations on your recent marriage," Micah said with equal parts sincerity and irony.

For a moment there was only the chorus of crickets in the long grass beyond the fence.

"It was a nice offer you made to Yasmine, but she doesn't need anything, so…" Remy's tone suggested Micah get very lost.

"I'll wait for her to tell me that herself. As I've been informed many times, women are allowed to make their own decisions, so…" *Bite me.*

They both took a long pull on their beer.

"Eden has low blood pressure," Micah thought to inform him. "If she gets dehydrated, she faints. On a day like today, put some pretzels or salted nuts in front of her."

"Aware," Remy said starkly. "She passed out on the beach and scared the hell out of me. It won't happen again." He jerked his chin toward the house. "If

Yasmine gives you something to wear, wear it. It hurts her feelings if you refuse. She's always right anyway. And you could afford to loosen up a notch." His side-eye hit Micah's tie.

It was his mother's birthday dinner. He had dressed appropriately. Although Remy did look comfortable yet smart in his raw linen shirt over striped trousers.

A burst of female laughter came from inside the house. They both glanced that direction.

"Never get between Eden and Quinn," Micah said gravely. He was doubly invested in that one.

Remy snorted. "I pity the fool who would think to try."

"Good answer."

They clinked their bottles and finished their beer in companionable silence.

CHAPTER TWELVE

LIKE ANY BRIDE, Quinn became so caught up in planning her wedding, dispensing with the vestiges of her life in Canada and securing a job, she overlooked the fact that she was completely changing her life. For a man. A man who didn't love her.

A man who was very, very different from her.

Reality began to crash back in around her when they arrived at the hotel in Wildenfels. It had actually been built as a Prussian palace and had housed eighteenth-century royalty. Part of it, a tower overlooking the courtyard, had been built in the 1200s. During Soviet times, the buildings and land had been used for collective farming. Later, it was renovated into apartment living, but as those units fell into disrepair, Micah's aunt had targeted it for purchase and redevelopment.

Over the last two years, marble floors had been uncovered, murals were cleaned, and plaster was restored. It was completely modernized, then decorated with crystal chandeliers, rococo-style furniture

and sumptuous bedding. The staff were suitably intimidated by the owner's arrival and eager to please.

Aside from a handful of intimate social engage-
ments, Quinn hadn't been out with Micah much.
They stayed in a lot, made love a *lot*, and it had
somehow slipped her mind that he was actually a
very well-known, wealthy and powerful man. When
it was just the two of them across a breakfast table,
she felt like equals.

They were not equals.

"It's not like this is our home," he dismissed when
she remarked on the opulence that surrounded them.
"It's an upscale hotel. It's supposed to impress."

"But you own it. And it's one property of many."
Hundreds?

He shrugged off her concern, saying that he
wanted to meet with the management team to ensure there would be no hiccups on their big day.

Quinn was left to change for greeting guests as
they arrived, but that was another mental wallop.

Much of her trousseau had been designed by Yasmine, but the list of items to include had been recommended by Eden. How had it become so many
outfits? She had a tea gown for their welcome reception, a little black dress for the cocktail mixer later,
then a dinner gown for the "intimate" family dinner
they would host tonight in a private dining room.

She had a negligee for tonight and a peignoir for
breakfast. In between, she had silk pajamas to wear
while getting ready and a "going away" outfit for the

end of the night. For the wedding, she had two different gowns! One was a simple satin crepe with organza-covered buttons down her back that she would wear for the civil ceremony. The other was a more elaborate A-line cut with a sweetheart neckline covered in appliqué lace that she would wear when they entered the reception. None of that included the two suitcases that were packed for their honeymoon.

Quinn had been happy with every single outfit because each felt like "her." They were simple and pretty and none were particularly ostentatious, but taken together the cost made her light-headed.

It was the vertigo of climbing far beyond her station in life. The fall from here would be catastrophic, and what was stopping her from falling?

The door opened and Micah startled her into hugging the beaded dress she was holding to her front.

"It occurred to me that we won't have a minute alone again until our honeymoon." He secured the lock and padded toward her like a jungle cat. "Would you like to enjoy one more hour of sin before we make this legal?"

She was so shaken by how swiftly she'd lost control of her life, her fingers went limp as he tugged the dress free of her grip. His mouth covered hers and she clasped onto what felt solid. Him.

Their tongues brushed and their groans of pleasure intermingled. He released a satisfied noise at her near-nakedness and cupped under her bottom, inviting her to leap onto him. She did, hugging him with her legs as he carried her to the bed.

It was like old times—almost frantic. As though time was limited. As though each time was the last time. *This* time felt like their last time.

"Quinn." He lifted his head once to look down at her, nostrils flared and cheeks flushed with lust. "What's wrong?"

"Nothing. I want this. I want you." She practically tore his buttons trying to open his shirt.

He popped them himself as he swept his hand down and yanked it free of his trousers. He tore the delicate French lace of her underwear rather than slide the silk down her thighs. His hand cupped her, hot and possessive.

"I love knowing this is all mine. Forever."

Her heart took a swerve at what she thought he almost said, I love... But he was kissing her again. Caressing her in a way he knew emptied her mind. They tangled tongues and she sucked on his bottom lip and scrambled to open his fly to take him in hand.

She was rushing both of them, she knew she was, but she needed to feel him *there*.

As she guided him, he rolled atop her, clothing in disarray, but still on. With a ragged noise, he gathered her beneath him and pressed.

She arched as she took him, savoring the slight sting as an echo of her distraught emotions.

"What's going on?" he asked gruffly as he smoothed her hair off her temple. "What do you need?"

"You. Just you." She swept her touch over every inch of bare skin she could access, inciting him to begin thrusting.

He kissed her again, deep and hot. His hips began a slow, powerful rhythm that made her groan. She felt his smile against the edge of her jaw.

"Shall we play our old game? How many times can I make you shatter before you destroy my control?"

Back then, their lovemaking had been a game. They'd been equal players locked in a sensual power struggle, playfully taunting each other with sensual caresses and teasing licks.

Today, he had the upper hand. She had given up her old life for him. She verged on taking his name and he even held her heart.

Recognizing that, she might have tried to hold something back, but she couldn't. She loved him too much. She clung to him and met his thrusts and let her cries of pleasure release with abandon. When he rolled onto his back, she rode him with fervor, grasping at his hands on her breasts and touching where they were joined. She met his narrowed gaze even though he must see into her soul. He must.

Time blurred and she lost track of how many times she shattered. When they were both stripped naked and lost to passion, all pretense at control completely lost, she let the truth spill from her lips.

"I love you."

He shouted with his release.

She joined him one last time.

* * *

Micah woke alone, which ticked him off. It was too much like their old pattern, him falling asleep after explosive sex, her slipping away while he snored off his orgasm.

Today had been different, though. Quinn had told him she loved him.

His heart lurched as the frantic edge on their love-making came back to him. When he'd returned to their suite, he'd expected a playful tumble, not such a torrid hour or this disturbing grit it had left in his breastbone.

Perhaps it had been the throes of passion, the same way he said things like *I love the way you taste*? She didn't expect him to say he believed in that emotion, now that she had agreed to marry him, did she?

His chest tightened at the thought. He valued honesty too much to lie to her, but that word was so ephemeral, yet loaded. *Love* wouldn't magically keep them together. Commitment would. He cared about her. She had to know that. Wasn't it enough?

She came out of the bathroom in a robe, bringing the humid fragrance of bodywash with her, but her hair was dry as she yanked the towel from her head. When she saw him, she halted abruptly, making him realize she'd been hurrying.

She had been trying to leave before he woke up!

Wordlessly, she veered to the mirrored dresser and picked up her hairbrush, wincing as she began running it through her hair. Her shoulder wasn't quite up to the task, but she did it as a sort of therapy.

"About what you said—" he began reluctantly.

"Ignore it. It didn't mean anything."

That landed like a mule kick in the chest. "Then why did you say it?"

"Let me rephrase," she turned to say hotly. "I meant it, but I know it didn't mean anything to you so forget I said it."

For three pulsebeats, he stared into the abyss that was her challenging expression. He saw the shadows of doubt and hurt flickering behind her eyes.

"I know you care about me, Quinn. We care about each other. That's as it should be."

The tendons in her neck flexed as though she was absorbing a blow. She looked away and slipped a mask over her face that he hadn't seen in a long time. It made a tremor start behind his heart, the first cracks of a long fracture.

"What does that word even do? It doesn't change anything. Do you think a man saying it would mean he's bringing more to the table than I am? Is he going to be more faithful than I am? Take better care of you when you're sick? We're a good match, Quinn."

"We absolutely are not." Her voice cut a low swath across the room. "Look around. Nothing in this room is mine."

As she looked around, vaguely frantic like someone waking from a dream and not fully comprehending reality, he realized they stood on very shaky ground.

"This is cold feet." He threw himself from the bed and stepped into his boxers. "These last weeks with you have been some of the happiest of my life." Not just because of the steady diet of sex—although he really enjoyed that. "I like having you in my life, Quinn. I like seeing you thrive."

She widened appalled eyes at him. "You like taking care of me."

"I do," he said without shame. "Because the opposite scenario, where you don't have what you need, makes me sick to think about." It wasn't like she was completely dependent on him. She'd just landed that job in Berlin and had blossomed with shy excitement at how much regard they had for her. He'd nearly died of pride.

Her cheeks were carved out so her cheekbones stood out starkly. Her eyes were bright.

"It does mean something to me that you would say those words. I know you wouldn't lie about something like that." He picked up her hand to kiss her fingers. They were cold and trembling.

He frowned and tried to warm them, but there was a knock at the door in the main room.

"Did you order room service?" he asked her.

"It's me," Eden called from behind the door.

Micah opened his mouth to say they were busy, but Quinn was already pulling her hand from his grip, hurrying to let her in.

With a light curse, he quickly found a robe in the bathroom and came back to the bedroom to see Eden pulling a dress from the closet.

"Oh, this is gorgeous. Quinn is coming to my room to get ready. Remy had to go to the airport to get Yasmine so we won't see them until the cocktail party. Vienna is on the same flight. Two fer one. But now that I've got you both…" Eden hugged Quinn's dress to her middle. "It's still early, but Remy said I could tell you since you'll be leaving for your honeymoon after tomorrow and I can't wait until—"

"Oh, Eden." Quinn rushed her, crushing the dress as she weepily embraced Eden.

"I know. I'm so happy!" Eden was teary as she held on to Quinn. Eden waved Micah to come into their hug.

"I'm happy for you," he said sincerely as he moved her hand from possibly putting too much pressure on Quinn's shoulder, then gently wrapped his arms around both of them. "For you and Remy," he assured her.

"Thank you. He's really happy, too." They all broke apart, but Eden poked him in the chest. "*Now* will you believe he's always been in love with me? And me with him?"

His head briefly swam, as though the rug had been pulled from beneath his feet. "I believe you believe you're in love. I believe you both want what's best for each other." As the words came out of his mouth, he could hear them striking Quinn at an angle, causing her to stiffen.

Quinn turned away to gather underthings and a pair of shoes.

"Quinn," he said.

"I'll see you downstairs." She threw a meaningless smile over her shoulder and left with Eden.

Quinn tried, she honestly tried not to cry, but as Eden was busy chattering about due dates and which room would be turned into a nursery, the pressure inside her just sputtered up and out.

"Quinn!"

"I'm sorry," she sobbed. "I want to be happy for you and I am. I swear I am."

"What happened? Just tell me what happened." Eden dropped everything to come sit beside her on the sofa.

"I love him. I told him I love him and he doesn't *care*. And now I've changed my whole life for him. Now I'm going to be a perpetual houseguest who brings nothing to his life and I can't walk away because he'll hate me and so will you!"

"I will never hate you. I will always love you," she soothed, gathering her into a hug. "You will always have me. Always, always. I should have come when you were in hospital. I knew that I should have, but I wanted to give you and Micah time. I thought... Well, I'm not going to make excuses for him. If he's broken your heart, he has to live with the consequences. Which includes the fact that he is dead to me."

"Don't say that, Eden." Quinn drew back and accepted the tissue Eden offered. "I was really mean to him when he didn't call you. I don't want to be the reason you two aren't getting along."

"But you are the reason. He's being an idiot."

"He's being honest! And I'm being selfish. He's a good person. I thought it was enough if I loved him. At least when it was in my head, I could convince myself we were both in love and not admitting it, but I *said* it. And now I know he doesn't love me and it hurts so much, Eden. So much more than I can stand. I don't know what to do."

"What do you want to do?"

"I just want to go home and…" She didn't even have a home. Fresh tears welled against her lashes. "But I can't walk away from my own wedding."

"Actually, you can. It's something people do now. Or so I've heard," Eden said with self-deprecation.

"I can't do that to him. I can't do it to you and your mom."

"Quinn." Eden took her hands. "You deserve to be loved. If he doesn't love you, then he doesn't deserve you."

Their first appearance was a tea reception on the terrace overlooking the pond, very casual. Summer was waning so it was a pleasant temperature with a hint of crispness on the air and an intense blue sky.

Micah and Quinn were supposed to be greeting guests with refreshments and conversation while staff hurried to register guests and take up their luggage.

She wasn't here. The longer he didn't see her, the more acutely his insides twisted with guilt and shame.

He'd hurt her. He had known he was hurting her as he was doing it and why? Why would he do that to someone he cared about?

Because to say he loved her would be to give her the power to hurt him. Devastating power.

His gaze drifted to where his mother spoke with an old friend, one he had deliberately invited so she would have some friendly faces here. That woman was highly influential. Even Aunt Zara would hesitate to get on her wrong side. His mother was smiling, but he recognized the tension in her. She was braced for having to face his father's family.

Nevertheless, she had come here for him. Because she loved him.

And he loved her. It had always been a very painful love, though. One filled with brief, happy reunions and too-soon goodbyes. It was the same with Eden. Love was always there, but it was rarely *here*.

Love was absence and pain. He was trying to spare Quinn. Didn't she see that?

But the pain had arrived regardless. If she wasn't with him, that's all he would ever feel. Pain.

* * *

Quinn finally found it. She'd gone through all the suitcases, but she'd finally found her hoodie.

She sank to the floor, still in the bathrobe she'd worn to Eden's room, and hugged the soft jersey to her chest. She hadn't wanted to leave without it, but now that she had it in her arms, she didn't know what to do.

That's how Micah found her.

The door into the suite opened and he called urgently, "Quinn."

He halted as he entered the bedroom, taking in the tossed suitcases.

He wore the shirt Yasmine had designed for him. Privately, he had told Quinn he wasn't sure about the burgundy pinstripes with the white tab collar, thinking it too casual for today, especially without a jacket, but matched with the merlot-colored tie and tie clip, he looked as polished as usual, with a bit more flair.

He crouched before her, brows pulled in anguish. "What are you doing?"

"I'm really tired of leaving without the things I love." Her eyes were dry, but stinging from all the tears she had shed. Her voice was hoarse. "Look. This has my name on it." She turned it over. "It's from my third year at university. My shoulder was bothering me so I asked the rowing team if I could dry-land-train with them. I knew my shoulder wasn't strong enough to row and compete, but they asked me to be their coxswain. We won a regatta, then everyone went their own ways, but I had this to prove that for that little while I belonged to something. I was wanted. Needed even."

"You're always wanted, Quinn." He shifted to sit, one knee bent, the other cocked. "I want you. Always. I'm not talking about sex. I'm talking about you. I want *you*. I need you. Do you understand that?"

She balled the hoodie in her lap, stomach churning with chagrin.

"Micah, I think I agreed to marry you because I wanted to be part of your family. I wanted to be Eden's sister-in-law and Lucille's daughter-in-law and finally be part of that."

"You *are* part of our family. I don't understand how you don't know how important you are to us. To *me*. Quinn, listen to me."

He shifted closer so he could take her hand. That's when he noticed her engagement ring was gone. He sucked in a breath and cradled her fist as though it was broken.

"If you don't want to marry me, Quinn, that's fine. It's fine. We can get past that, but don't leave me, Quinn. You can't…" An agonized flinch flexed across his expression. "I can't keep saying goodbye to the people I love."

She gasped and tried to take back her hand, but he held on.

"I tried not to love you because I knew that if

you ever walked away—and you always walk away, Quinn…" His voice shook with accusation while his brows crashed down. His hand closed over hers, not hard, but squeezing enough to transmit his agony. "I knew if you left me for good, it would be more than I could take. So I tried not to love you. I tried to let it be what you seemed to want because at least I understood that kind of relationship. But I *do* love you, Quinn. It scares the hell out of me how much I love you."

"You don't have to keep saying it if—"

"Don't you dare throw it back on me. You wanted this, Quinn. Now you take it, same as I have to. We love each other. We have to watch the other person hold our heart and it's going to hurt. Loving hurts. It makes you vulnerable and when they hurt, you hurt. When they're lying in a hospital bed, you wonder if you'll have any reason to live tomorrow. But when they're happy…" He lifted his gaze from where he was abrading the back of her hand with the restless rub of his thumb. "When you are happy, Quinn, I don't need air or water. I want you with me and I want to see you smile. Is that too much to ask?"

She wasn't smiling right now. Tears were running down her cheeks as she reached toward something she wanted so badly, she didn't know if she would topple or finally touch it.

"I'm really scared, Micah. I love you *so much*. I wanted to leave, but I wanted my sweater. Then when I found it…" She looked down at it in her lap.

"It's not enough anymore, to only have a memory of belonging once. I want to really belong. Forever. I want to belong with you." It shook her very foundations to ask for that.

"You do," he promised solemnly. "We belong together whether we marry or not. I think that's been true for a very long time."

"Yeah," she agreed, sagging with relief. She let the last of her defenses fall and tried to find a smile, but her lips were still quivery. "I just didn't know what it looked like to belong with someone, so I didn't recognize it when it happened."

"Same." He gathered her closer and touched his unsteady smile to hers. "But now I know it looks like red hair and freckles."

"And sounds like sarcasm," she tacked on.

"I'm not being sarcastic." He drew back from his almost-kiss and gave her a disgruntled frown.

"No, I was saying that I'm sarcastic and I belong with—oh, never mind. If it takes too long to explain, it's not a clever joke. Will you kiss me? Please? You promised that no matter how badly we fought, I could always ask you for what I need."

"Yes, but you have to come all the way into my lap because that's what *I* need right now. And promise me that if you ever do leave, I'll be the thing you wreck a bedroom looking for, so you can take me with you."

"Or I could stay and wreck a bedroom with you,"

she suggested as she nestled close, one arm behind his back and the other twining around his neck.

"Wrecking a bedroom together will always be my preference. Now stop talking. I have a kiss to deliver."

"I really do love you, though. You know that, don't you?" she asked anxiously.

"I do know that. Now tell me you know I love you. That the knowledge and belief is all the way in here where it can never be doubted or get misplaced." He touched the middle of her chest.

His touch seemed to light a glow inside her, one that grew hot and bright under the fierce light in his eyes. It dispelled old shadows of doubts and warmed all her cold corners of loneliness. There was no hesitation in her as she accepted it. She deserved this, deserved him. She deserved love.

And she had *his* love, which was extra special for its rarity and strength.

"I do," she vowed.

EPILOGUE

THEY MARRIED AN hour later at the registrar's office.

Micah left the decision to Quinn whether they would go through with it or simply live together for the rest of their lives.

Quinn chose to marry him. She wanted the commitment, not because she doubted either of their steadfastness, but because it cemented where they belonged—with each other. Also, she really, really didn't want to put Lucille through watching another of her children cancel a wedding.

Micah assured her that his mother would understand, but he also leaped on calling the registrar's office to ask if they had an opening today.

"We have that many dinners and socials to get through, you might change your mind again," he joked, holding the phone to his chest. "What do you say?"

"I say 'yes.'" She rose from the bed and put on her engagement ring from the dish where she'd left it. "But I won't have time to do that dress justice."

She wore her blue hoodie. Micah left off his tie and didn't bother shaving so he had a hint of shadow around his jaw.

It was short and sweet and when they were pronounced husband and wife, he kissed her reverently. Then he held on to her for a long time. His heart crashed against hers and his mouth rested against her hair.

"This is genuinely the happiest day of my life," he told her in a quiet rasp.

When they finally drew back, she smiled her biggest smile at him. He cupped her face, and his eyes were wet with happy tears.

They spent the evening making appearances with their guests, the only hiccup when Quinn had to head off Eden as she bore down on her brother, ready to take a strip off him.

"Look. Shh… We have a secret of our own." Quinn showed her the second ring she wore.

Eden cried, of course, and hugged her hard.

The rest of the celebrations went ahead as scheduled. It was like a fairy tale, one that Quinn would look back on and marvel at, partly because it was so movie-perfect, but more because her husband made her feel so loved. He didn't make any grand gestures. No, it was in the quiet touch on her back and the meeting of her gaze that told her she was precious. It was the way he looked for her when she returned to a room and the way he absently centered her rings when he held her hand. It was in the way they made love that night, with their whole hearts open, sealing their love for all time.

It was frightening to believe she was wanted and needed and loved this much, but hour by hour and day by day, her trust in what they had grew. Month by month, she turned each of their houses into a home. They were building a life together that was solid and secure, everything she had ever needed.

Then, one day, shortly after their second anniversary, Quinn came home to tell him with soft solemnity, "I think I met our daughter today."

Micah pushed away from his desk. "Tell me."

They had already begun the process of becoming foster parents. Quinn had dropped some certified documents at the agency and had glimpsed a five-year-old girl holding a brand-new teddy bear. There'd been a half-stuffed garbage bag at her feet.

"Her foster mother had a family emergency. It was Abigail's third house in two years."

Abigail came into their home a few weeks later. She was shy and polite and didn't mention that her shoes were too tight. Micah noticed when he was helping her struggle to get them on. He immediately took her to buy new ones, which made her cry, because she didn't want to give up her old ones. She loved them too much.

A special trunk was procured for items that meant a lot to her. She flourished, and soon Abigail was offering her items from the trunk to other children, secure that she had all she needed in the vast, enduring love of her parents.

* * * * *

If you got swept up in
A Convenient Ring to Claim Her
then you'll love the other instalments in the
Four Weddings and a Baby *miniseries*
Cinderella's Secret Baby
Wedding Night with the Wrong Billionaire
And don't miss the fourth instalment,
coming soon!

Meanwhile, why not explore more stories
from Dani Collins?

Married for One Reason Only
Manhattan's Most Scandalous Reunion
One Snowbound New Year's Night
Cinderella for the Miami Playboy
Innocent in Her Enemy's Bed

Available now!

#4089 THE BABY THE DESERT KING MUST CLAIM
by Lynne Graham

When chef Claire is introduced to her elusive employer, she gets the shock of her life! Because the royal that Claire has been working for is Raif, father to the baby Claire's *just* discovered she's carrying!

#4090 A SECRET HEIR TO SECURE HIS THRONE
by Caitlin Crews

Grief-stricken Paris Apollo is intent on getting revenge for his parents' deaths. And he's just discovered a shocking secret: his son! A legitimate heir will mean a triumphant return to power—*if* Madelyn will marry him...

#4091 BOUND BY THE ITALIAN'S "I DO"
A Billion-Dollar Revenge
by Michelle Smart

Billionaire Gianni destroyed Issy's family legacy. Now, it's time for payback by taking down his company! Then Gianni calls her bluff with an outrageous marriage proposal. And Issy must make one last move...by saying *yes!*

#4092 HIS INNOCENT FOR ONE SPANISH NIGHT
Heirs to the Romero Empire
by Carol Marinelli

Alej's desire for photographer Emily is held at bay solely by his belief she's too innocent for someone so cynical. Until one passionate encounter becomes irresistible! The trouble is, now Alej knows exactly how electric they are together...

#4093 THE GREEK'S FORGOTTEN MARRIAGE
by Maya Blake

Imogen has finally tracked down her missing husband, Zeph. But he has no recollection of their business-deal union! Yet as Zeph slowly pieces his memories together, one thing is for certain: this time, an on-paper marriage won't be enough!

#4094 RETURNING FOR HIS RUTHLESS REVENGE
by Louise Fuller

When self-made Gabriel hires attorney Dove, it's purely business—unfinished business, that is. Years ago, she broke his heart...now he'll force her to face him! Yet their chemistry is undeniable. Will they finally finish what they started?

#4095 RECLAIMED BY HIS BILLION-DOLLAR RING
by Julia James

It's been eight years since Nikos left Calanthe without a goodbye. Now, becoming the Greek's bride is the only way to help her ailing father. Even if it feels like she's walking back into the lion's den...

#4096 ENGAGED TO LONDON'S WILDEST BILLIONAIRE
Behind the Palace Doors...
by Kali Anthony

Lance's debauched reputation is the stuff of tabloid legend. But entertaining thoughts of his attraction to sheltered Sara would be far too reckless. Then she makes him an impassioned plea to help her escape an arranged wedding. His solution? Their own headline-making engagement!

HARLEQUIN
PLUS

Try the best multimedia subscription service for romance readers like you!

Read, Watch and Play.

Experience the easiest way to get the romance content you crave.

Start your **FREE TRIAL** at
www.harlequinplus.com/freetrial.